Genius under Construction

Genius under construction

By Marilee Haynes

Pauline
BOOKS & MEDIA
Boston

Library of Congress Cataloging-in-Publication Data

Haynes, Marilee.
  Genius under construction / by Marilee Haynes.
    pages cm
  Sequel to: a.k.a. genius.
  Summary: "Eighth-grade genius Gabe discovers how his giftedness can serve others"– Provided by publisher.
  ISBN-13: 978-0-8198-3126-2
  ISBN-10: 0-8198-3126-3
  [1. Genius–Fiction. 2. Gifted children–Fiction. 3. Catholic schools–Fiction. 4. Middle schools–Fiction. 5. Schools–Fiction.] I. Title.
  PZ7.H3149146Ge 2014
  [Fic]–dc23

                               2013031122

This is a work of fiction. Names, characters, places, events, and incidents are either the products of the author's imagination or used in a fictitious manner. Any resemblance to actual persons, living or dead, or actual events is purely coincidental.

Many manufacturers and sellers distinguish their products through the use of trademarks. Any trademarked designations that appear in this book are used in good faith but are not endorsed by, authorized by, associated with, or sponsored by the trademark owners.

Cover design by Mary Joseph Peterson, FSP

Cover art by Tracy Hill

"P" and PAULINE are registered trademarks of the Daughters of St. Paul.

Published by Pauline Books & Media, 50 Saint Paul's Avenue, Boston, MA 02130-3491

Printed in the U.S.A.

GUC VSAUSAPEOILL11-2710011 3126-3

www.pauline.org

Pauline Books & Media is the publishing house of the Daughters of St. Paul, an international congregation of women religious serving the Church with the communications media.

1 2 3 4 5 6 7 8 9   18 17 16 15 14

For my husband

— Love always

One

It's here. The first day of eighth grade. My last year at St. Jude Middle School. I'm still mostly the same me I was on the last day of seventh grade. Still kind of short. Still more than kind of smart. And still completely confused by girls.

There's nothing I can do about the short part—I checked. And the smart part is mostly okay. But the girls part. I have a plan for that—avoid them as much as possible.

That's the *what* of the plan, anyway. It's the *how* part that's a little fuzzy. Because out of the 314 students at St. Jude Middle School, 183 are girls. That's 58.28%. More than half. So avoiding them could be a problem. And as any engineer would tell you, every plan, no matter how well designed, has problems—or obstacles. The biggest—and loudest—obstacle to my plan sits next to me, almost shoulder to shoulder.

"We're here. Can you believe we're actually here?" Linc says for at least the seventeenth time. This time he mixes it up by elbowing me hard in what would be my bicep if I had one. All of a sudden he does have biceps—and triceps and pecs and other muscle-like things that mean he's stronger and also a little more dangerous to sit next to than he used to be.

"Of course I can believe it. We've been here for seventy-nine minutes now. Which, by the way, is more than enough time for both my butt cheeks to go completely numb." It's also more than enough time for my hair to double in size since it's August and the humidity is 87% and, well, that's what my hair does.

"I know, but it's so worth it."

And the truth is he's right. Because for the first time ever, we're sitting on "the rock." The enormous rock in front of school that only eighth graders can sit on. It's some kind of St. Jude Academy Middle School rule—unofficial, of course—that goes back to the dark ages even before my dad was a student here. And because Linc is Linc, he said we had to be first this year. And because Linc has been my best friend for as long as I can remember—

and because he bugged me about it every day for the entire summer—I said yes. Even though it meant getting up earlier than any person should actually ever get up for school. We did. And we got here first. And even though sitting here for this long is totally uncomfortable—it *is* a rock, after all—it's also kind of awesome.

"Hey, who's the cute girl with Maya?"

Again with the elbow. I rub the sore spot on my arm and turn my head in the direction Linc is pointing to. There's Maya. And Linc's right, there is a girl with her. A girl I've never seen before with light brown hair that swings from side to side when she walks.

"Don't really know. She said something about Mrs. Capistrano calling and asking her to help with some new students."

By the time I'm done talking, Maya and the girl with the swingy hair are standing in front of us.

"And this is the rock. People paint it during the year—usually for birthdays or if some team wins a big game. But only eighth graders can sit on it. It's like a school law or something." Maya rolls her eyes and the other girl giggles. Maya is acting like she doesn't see us sitting there. And since I'm supposed to be avoiding girls (even if my plan doesn't technically include Maya since she's supposed to be my second-best friend), I don't say anything either. But Linc is definitely not avoiding girls.

3

"Hi, Maya. Hi, person with Maya. I'm Lincoln Jefferson Truman, but you can call me Linc." Linc reclines a little and smiles big enough to show all his teeth.

Swingy-hair-girl giggles again. Maya blows her bangs up out of her eyes. "Yeah, that's Linc and the other one is Gabe. This is Shelby. She's new."

Before I have to say anything, the bell rings. Linc and I slide off the rock and head toward the front doors with Maya and Shelby. Linc and Shelby are talking—well, Linc is talking and Shelby is giggling. I mostly concentrate on walking as normally as possible despite the fact that I still can't feel my butt.

First-day-of-school sounds bounce down and around the hallway—the yelling, the whooping, the slamming of bodies into lockers (some people have a really weird way of being happy to see each other after summer vacation).

I square my shoulders and face my locker, head on. I check the slip of paper with my combination. I've got this. Breathe in, breathe out, and go—27 right, 12 left, 2 right. Listen for the click and lift. It opens. I shrug like it's no big deal even as a sigh of relief seeps out of me bit by bit. Because out of the first 107 days of seventh grade, my locker opened exactly two times. And even though it opened every one of the last 73 days of seventh grade and this is a totally different locker in a totally different hallway, there was no way to know if the locker magic would keep over the summer. Looks like it did. Bonus.

Since I only grew 3/8 of an inch over the summer, which is completely undetectable to anyone or anything, I affix my new locker mirror at the exact same latitude as my last year's locker mirror. Everyone has one and everyone says they're for checking hair. For some kids, they probably are. But my hair is my hair and looking at it isn't going to change it, so I mostly use mine to check for boogers in my nose or food in my teeth. All clear.

I line up my books on the shelf in the order I'll need them, then pull the first one back out and load it into my bag along with a fresh notebook, my lucky Superman pen and two spares. A lot of people—Linc—don't think it's important to always have a spare pen, but then a lot of people—Linc—always end up asking me for a pen when they forget one or when the one old, chewed-on, nasty pen they do have runs out of ink.

Last year I had a backpack on wheels that I dragged everywhere I went. This was because the whole locker-that-I-could-never-get-open problem meant I had to have all my books with me all the time. This year instead of a backpack, rolling or otherwise, I'm using my grandpa's briefcase. It's old and soft and the leather still smells the tiniest bit like him. My grandma gave it to me after—well, after everything. After I sling the long strap of the bag across my body, I trace his initials on the front for luck.

Two

Here it is. The Clubhouse. One-time meeting place of the Wednesday Weather Club until it died from lack of members (it was just me and Linc, and he only came because I promised good snacks) and current home of G.A.S. class.

Greater Achieving Students (G.A.S.) was just one of the things that happened because of the whole "hey, all of a sudden I'm a genius" thing last year. It ended up being one of the better things. Most of it, anyway. It's the reason there's a trophy in the trophy case that I helped put there and it was a big part of why seventh grade ended up being pretty good. I'm hoping for more of the same for eighth grade. No big changes. No big surprises.

And after what happened with Becca Piccarelli, no girls. It's all part of the plan.

"Gabe—wait up!" Linc weaves his way down the hall, barely avoiding running people over.

The bell rings just as we get to the door. And on the other side of the door is the first surprise of the day. Sister Stevie. She stands there looking a lot like she did last year. Same long white dress, same black veil sitting crookedly on her crayon-yellow hair. Same high-top sneakers—hot pink ones. Same happy-to-see-you smile.

"Gabe. Linc. Come in. Sit down."

Linc and I snag the same seats as last year, me by the window and Linc next to me. This year there are more desks. Seats for ten students instead of just six. Some of them are already full. There's Shelby, the new girl with the swingy hair, and Cameron Goodrich, the only person I've ever punched. Well, other than Maya, but that was an accident. And it was Cameron's fault.

I see a couple of seventh graders I know—including Mary Frances Gonzales. Ever since her picture was in the paper a few years ago for winning the library's summer reading challenge—she read more pages than any other kid in the state of North Carolina (and probably the world)—she acts like she's famous. She's not. But she is sitting behind me. When class starts, there's still one empty desk.

Maya's in her same-as-last-year spot on the other end, her hand already waving in the air. Class hasn't even started and she already has a question. The thing is, so do I.

"Yes, Maya?" says Sister Stevie.

"What are you doing here? I thought you weren't coming back."

That was my question, too. Because Sister Stevie being our teacher was supposed to be a one-time kind of thing. A just-last-year thing. She said good-bye to us at the end of seventh grade and cried and everything. We even got her flowers and a card—a mushy goodbye card my mom picked out.

"I know. I have so much to tell you." Sister Stevie grabs the giant exercise ball she uses instead of a chair and settles herself on it, facing the two semicircles of desks. She smiles big enough to show the dimples in both her cheeks and claps her hands like a little kid.

"See, after the school year ended, I went back to teaching college classes. Summer classes. And it was fine. But I realized something important." Sister bounces on the ball hard enough to almost shake her veil loose. "I liked teaching all of you better. So I prayed about it—a lot—and got permission from my Mother Superior. Then I called Mr. Dooley and convinced him that he needed me. That you needed me, too. I prayed a bunch more while he thought about it and—*ta da*—I'm back. I'll be teaching both this class and eighth grade religion."

I look over at Linc, who is doing something really weird. Instead of slouching way down in his seat and doodling or chewing on his pen or doing any of the other things Linc usually does in class, he's sitting up straight and facing Sister Stevie. The notebook on his desk looks almost new and he's even—wait, is he really? He is. He's taking notes. I poke my leg out to the left and kick his chair. He doesn't even flinch. Weirder than weird.

Sister Stevie keeps talking about how happy she is to be back and how much fun we're going to have this year. I take a break from listening to her and looking at the weirdness of Linc paying attention to check out the skies. When I crane my neck over to the side as far as it will reach, I see the same thing I saw this morning. Pure Carolina blue sky, not even one cloud to look at. Nothing to give a clue about what might come later.

The back and forth of Sister Stevie and Maya's voices goes on and on. It's a full-on Maya-Ling-style inquisition and it lasts until the bell rings. Day one of G.A.S. class is over.

"See you this afternoon, Gabe," says Sister Stevie on my way out.

I raise my eyebrows and one of my shoulders to say "see you later" without actually having to say it.

Sister Stevie being back is kind of great. I mean, I like her more than I've liked any teacher in a long time. But it's also kind of *not* great because Sister Stevie has a way of making everything be about more than what it seems to be. She makes kids think about things and stretch their brains in directions where maybe some people's brains (like mine) might not be made to stretch.

"I can't believe I overlooked the possibility of a cute new girl." Linc smacks himself in the forehead and passes me the basketball.

"What are you talking about?"

"I mean, all summer I thought about who might show up on the first day of school a lot cuter than she was when she left on the last day. You know, who might get her braces off or magically have her skin clear up. I narrowed my list down to the six most likely candidates. I was right, by the way. But the new-girl thing totally slipped my mind." Again with a forehead smack. He's going to knock his brain loose. Looser than it already is.

"What new girl?"

"Shelby Frasier. Shelby with the swinging hair and the great smile. Shelby who's in our G.A.S. class and laughs at everything I say."

"Oh, her. It's not really a laugh. It's a giggle. And don't you think it's kind of annoying?" Because I do.

"Annoying? You're just saying that because she doesn't think you're funny," says Linc. He motions for me to take a shot.

Since I have nothing more to say on the subject of Shelby the giggling new girl, I step into position.

Woomp, woomp, woomp. Stop, aim, and shoot. Clang. Off the rim. And I missed. Again.

"That's M." Linc uses his T-shirt to wipe the worst of the sweat from his face, dribbles twice, and takes a jump shot. Swish.

Two more letters and I'll have H-I-P-P-O-P-O-T-A-M-U-S. Then I can sit down and guzzle water until I stop feeling like I'm going to burst into flames. It might be the first day of school but it's still August. And August in North Carolina means two things—high temperatures and even higher humidity. Ugh.

This time I skip the dribbling, the stopping, and the aiming. Linc and I both know I stink at jump shots. I just shoot. Big surprise, it doesn't go in. That's U. Today I wish we still played H-O-R-S-E. It'd already be over.

I dream about cold things while Linc decides what his next shot will be. A double scoop of pistachio almond fudge ice cream on a waffle cone. Yum. Cirrocumulus clouds—they always mean cold weather. Snow—like last Christmas Eve. I try to remember how it felt when my "little" sister Sabrina stuffed a snowball down the neck of my jacket. In the middle of almost remembering, a giant drop of sweat forms in my hair, travels down my forehead and through my eyebrow until it lands in my right eye.

While I'm trying to figure out a way to make my head stop sweating so much, the basketball hits me in the chest. Linc's standing just behind the free-throw line we drew with chalk. By the showing-all-his-teeth smile on his face, I know he just made another basket.

Fine. A free throw. The one shot I know I can make—at least I know I can make it with 72.8% accuracy. If I shoot it underhand. Granny style. I've got the stats to prove it. But it's so hot. And there's a bottle of ice cold water waiting in the fridge. So I do the only thing I can do. The smart thing. I walk over and take the shot overhand. I miss.

"That's S," I say. "Water break."

Linc whoops and high fives himself like he doesn't beat me every time we play H-I-P-P-O-P-O-T-A-M-U-S.

By the time I get back with our waters, he's done celebrating.

We sit side by side against the garage door in the one sliver of shade on the driveway and gulp our water. After we burp two huge burps—Linc's is louder, longer, and smells like a tuna fish sandwich mixed with sweaty socks—Linc grabs my notebook and starts flipping through the pages.

"Hey, is this right?" he asks.

"What do you mean?"

"Is this right? Am I as good as these other guys?"

"That's what I told you. Your shot stats are better than all but two of the guys on last year's team. And one of them was Ty. Since he graduated that makes you better than all but one."

After I used my project for the Academic Olympics to prove to Ty Easterbrook, star of last year's St. Jude basketball team, that shooting free throws granny style leads to more points, better stats, and more wins, some people started listening to what I had to say about basketball. Since I stink at actually playing basketball, it was kind of weird and completely awesome at the same time.

Linc stays quiet for a long time. His mouth's not moving, his arms and legs are still, and he barely seems to be breathing.

"You okay?" I ask.

Instead of answering my question, he turns to me and says, "So if I tried out for the team, do you think I'd make it?"

It's an easy question to answer. Sort of. "Well, yeah. Of course you'd make it. But . . ."

"Yeah, but . . ."

The "but" is Linc's parents. They think school is for school and not for sports. They're both doctors and want him to be one, too. But Linc's grades aren't what anybody would call great. Especially Dr. and Dr. Truman. So whenever he asks if he can join a team, the answer is "no." I secretly think that even if his grades *were* great, the answer would still be "no."

"So I've been working on something." Linc's expression is so serious it almost doesn't look like his face at all.

"Yeah?"

"I put together something for my mom and dad. Kind of like a proposal. I gave a bunch of reasons why they should let me try out for the team and promised to do some stuff better at school."

"Is that why you were paying attention in G.A.S. class?"

"Yep." Linc smiles, jumps up, and starts dribbling the ball. "Who knows, if I try really hard I might even end up being as smart as you."

"It could happen." I cross my eyes and he laughs. Linc's really happy, but I feel like I have to ask. "Um, do you really think they might say yes?" What I don't say is that every other time—every single time—they've said "no."

Linc doesn't answer until after he's made four baskets in a row from all over the driveway.

"I don't know. But I've got to try."

Aim. Shoot. Swish.

Three

I slap my algebra book closed and flex my left hand a few times to get the blood flowing again. Back to school for a week and the teachers are already trying to bury us in homework. The aroma of baking cookies hits the olfactory receptors in my nose, triggering my brain to decide it's time for a post-study snack. My growling stomach agrees.

I walk into the kitchen in time to see Mom slide fresh cookies onto the rack to cool. I close my eyes and give a huge sniff. Chocolate. Vanilla. And something nutty.

"What kind are they?" I ask.

"Chocolate chunk with macadamia nuts."

Yum. Actually, double yum. I plop onto a stool at the

counter and Mom puts two cookies on a plate for me with an apple. I take a giant bite out of the apple. Eating it first is the only way to avoid a mom-lecture on the importance of a balanced diet.

"How'd the homework go? All finished?"

Since my mouth is full I roll my shoulders around and then nod to mean "it went okay" and "yes."

Mom plops more dough onto a cookie sheet while I plow through the rest of my snack. The only sound in the kitchen is my chewing—with my mouth closed, of course.

"These are so good," I say after I swallow the last bite. "New recipe?"

My mom started her cookie business, Heavenly Bites, when I started kindergarten. Having a mom who bakes cookies every day is definitely not the worst thing that could happen to a guy.

"Yep. I added more chocolate chips and vanilla than usual and roasted the macadamia nuts first."

Whatever she did, it worked. I go after the crumbs on my plate with my finger—these cookies are too delicious to leave even one particle uneaten.

"Gabe?" When I look up, my mom is holding something behind her back and wearing an expression on her face I can't quite figure out. She almost looks guilty but there's a smile on top of it. One of those fake smiles like when she tries to convince me that cleaning my room will be fun.

"What?"

"I found something today when I was looking for things to donate to the yard sale at church. This was in your closet."

She slides the thing she's been holding behind her back across the counter. It's a thick, dark blue envelope and it's addressed to me.

"You found this in my closet?"

"Yes."

"In my closet under a pile of LEGO boxes, socks that probably smelled bad, and some old shoes?"

"Really smelly socks, actually, and also the crust of an old peanut butter and jelly sandwich that had started growing things. Yes."

"Isn't that snooping?"

As soon as the words are out of my mouth, I know I shouldn't have said them. After I sit through a lecture on rights and privacy and how kids—even if they are now teenagers and actually especially now that they are teenagers—aren't entitled to either when it comes to their own homes and their own rooms, I flip the envelope over so my name isn't staring at me.

"Honey, the envelope hadn't even been opened." But it was open now. "It's your application."

My application.

"Gabe, what's going on?"

I'm saved from answering a question that I don't actually have an answer for by the arrival of my pain-in-the-everything sister Sabrina. She's crying. Again.

"Sabrina, honey, what's wrong?" asks my mom.

Sabrina just sobs louder and flings herself into my mom's arms. Mom staggers a little—Sabrina's now taller than she is—and then starts petting my sister's hair like you'd pet a dog if you had one. We don't.

"Okay, now what is it?" Mom says after the sobs go down about twenty decibels in volume.

Sabrina leans back. "Just look."

I glance at her and see my same-as-always irritating, dramatic, one-year-younger-but-still-taller-than-me sister. My mom must see something else, because she says, "Oh, Sabrina. It's not that bad."

"Yes, it is. It's huge. And it's right on the end of my nose. I can't go to school tomorrow. I just can't." The sobbing ratchets up again—louder this time.

I study her face more closely this time and now I see what she's talking about. It's a zit. And yes, it is on the tip of her nose. And while I wouldn't call it huge, I would call it something you wouldn't want to walk around with on your face.

Ever since the beginning of summer, Sabrina has been more of a pain than ever. My mom said something about "changes" and then she took Sabrina out for a special day of shopping and lunch at a fancy restaurant. Whatever. But ever since Sabrina "changed," there's been a lot more crying and door slamming and a lot more of her blaming me for everything and anything that goes wrong in her annoying twelve-year-old life.

"Come on, honey. Let's go into my bathroom. I'll show you how to make it disappear with a little concealer. No one will even notice it," says Mom.

A not-quite-quiet-enough snort comes out before I can stop it.

"Mo-om! Make him stop." Sabrina stomps her foot and wails some more.

"Gabe." Mom's knock-it-off voice means I'd better not disobey.

"Sorry." I shrug and turn away, hatching a plan to snag two more cookies while my mom deals with Sabrina and her zit.

"I noticed the deadline on that application is eight weeks from tomorrow, and the entrance exam is even sooner. There's still plenty of time, but you'll have to get on it right away. We'll talk about this more when Dad gets home."

"Um . . ."

"Oh, and Gabe, no more cookies."

As soon as I walk into my room, I settle onto the middle of my bed and stare at the envelope. It has my name and address in the *to* part and "Carolina Science and Math High School" in the *from* part. It's a school that specializes in teaching math, science, engineering, and technology. In other words, all the stuff I care about. It's also a place I always thought I'd go to high school. And I wasn't the only one who thought so.

Carolina Science and Math High School (CSMHS) was a me-and-Grandpa thing. But him dying last year means there is no me and Grandpa anymore. So now it's just a me thing.

Getting into CSMHS is hard. Really hard. There are a bunch of steps. And at every one of them, there's a chance of getting a "no." It takes a lot of "yeses" to actually get to go there—four to be exact. But it only takes one "no" to knock you out of the running.

That's why I didn't open the envelope. It could have been a "no." CSMHS only invites certain middle school students to apply. You tell your school counselor that you want to apply and they ask CSMHS if you can. I told Mrs. Capistrano last year—before Grandpa died. She told them after. Then people there check out your grades and a bunch of other stuff about you. Nobody knows exactly what. And sometimes—actually lots of times—they say "no." They won't even let you apply. Grandpa used to say, "They know what they're looking for." But what if they weren't looking for me?

So when I found the envelope in the mailbox ten days ago, I decided to wait to find out if it was a "yes" or a "no." Just for a little while. That's why I stuffed it behind a bunch of stuff I thought was either too old or too gross for my mom. Wrong.

I try to ignore the clenching feeling in my stomach that's back for the first time since last year as I pull an application out of the envelope. There's a letter addressed to me, too, officially inviting me to apply. This is a big deal. It's a "yes."

That makes one.

Four

This year, my locker is right across the hall from the nook where the statue of Saint Jude hangs out. Saint Jude, the patron saint of lost causes. In other words, the perfect person to watch over a bunch of kids trying to survive middle school. I hope I don't need him as much as I did last year, but it's still nice to have him close by.

So on the way to G.A.S. class, I swing by to say hey to Saint Jude and offer up a quick prayer asking for some help with this whole application situation. I don't wait around for an answer. That's not how it works.

When I get to G.A.S. class, I slip in the door and head for my desk. Halfway there I stop and stare at something I've never seen before.

It's Linc. And he's already at his desk, which has never happened. Never. Not only that, but on his desk are a notebook open to a fresh page and a pen—his own, non-chewed-on pen—uncapped and ready to go. He's not even talking to Shelby. Linc's ignoring a cute girl sitting right next to him. A cute girl who's smiling and swinging her hair in his direction. It's like someone else has taken over his body. Of course I know that's a scientific impossibility, but that doesn't make what's going on any less weird.

"Okay, everyone sit down and get ready."

Since I'm the only one still standing, I guess she means me. I slide the rest of the way across the room and collapse into my seat. Sister Stevie starts talking before my butt has a chance to find the lone comfortable spot on my chair.

"Those of you who were with me last year know that I like to ask you to stretch your brains." She grins and settles onto the big blue ball. "And sometimes that means doing things that make you feel a little bit uncomfortable—like writing and reciting poetry."

Sister Stevie's gaze lands on me. I hold my breath and hope that she's not going to ask me to recite the poem I wrote last year about the different areas of scientific study. I did my best to wipe that memory from my brain right after it happened. She stares at me just long enough to make me think she's going to, which is also just long enough for the clenching in my stomach to start.

"Linc, what do you think of when you think about math?"

The relief I feel when Sister moves on to Linc makes me relax. Too much. The clenching in my stomach is gone, but the reason it's gone sneaks out into the classroom with a squeak. A squeak I try to cover by coughing, but there's no mistaking that someone just farted. And that someone was me. My nervous stomach is back.

Mary Frances Gonzales's "Eww" is loud enough for everyone to hear.

Linc directs a hand fart in my direction before answering. "Numbers?" Everyone laughs. I guess that answers my whole body snatchers question. He's still Linc.

"Yes, of course. But what else?"

"Um, I guess one right answer. Yeah, that's it. In math there's only one right answer." Linc scratches his pit and scrunches up his face. "And sometimes it's really hard to find it."

The one-right-answer thing is what I like best about math.

"But that's the best part." It's Cameron, saying the same thing I was thinking. Cameron and I being on the same side of anything is almost as weird as Linc paying attention.

"I agree with both of you." Sister Stevie looks around the room and stops on Shelby. "How about art? Shelby, what do you think of when you think about art?"

"Um, beauty? And, you know, feelings and stuff?" Shelby swings her hair back and forth and back again. "I guess I just like art, a lot?" She giggles after she's done talking.

Why does everything Shelby says sound like a question? And why does she giggle so much?

"Exactly. Art makes you feel," says Sister Stevie. The hair swinging and giggling stop. "It can make you feel happy or sad or angry or excited or confused or peaceful or anything else you can think of."

"So we're going to study art?" asks Maya. I don't have to look at her to know she doesn't think this is a good idea.

"You're half-right," says Sister. "This quarter, we're going to study art and math." She bounces twice and stands up. "Art and math together."

Huh?

"Art and math don't go together." Maya sounds as sure as sure can be.

"Yeah, they do."

All of our heads, including Sister Stevie's, turn toward the door. Our principal, Mr. Dooley, stands in the doorway with a kid who looks like he got lost on the way to third grade. He grins and pushes his glasses back up his nose.

"Mr. Dooley?" Sister Stevie stands up and walks over to the door.

"Sister, this is Spencer Trask. He's the student I was telling you about."

"But I thought . . ."

Whatever Sister Stevie thought is going to stay a mystery—at least to us. She clamps her lips shut, closes her eyes for a second, and then gives Spencer one of her biggest, dimpliest smiles.

"Change in plans, Sister," says Mr. Dooley. "Spencer is joining us early. Today in fact."

"Welcome, Spencer. I'm Sister Stevie. And this is the rest of the class. If you'd like to take a seat, we'll continue our discussion. It sounds like you might have some things to add."

Spencer hops into the seat behind Maya that's been empty since school started two weeks ago. His feet barely touch the ground. How old is this kid? And why is he here?

I can tell Sister Stevie wants Mr. Dooley to leave so she can get back to teaching. Probably everyone in the room can tell. Everyone except Mr. Dooley.

"Now some of you probably recognize Spencer," he says.

All of our heads turn and take another look. I see what I saw when he walked in. A skinny little kid with dark brown skin and super-short curly hair. His green polo shirt—our school uniform—swallows the top half of his body. I don't think I've seen him before.

"Were you on Super Quiz Masters Junior?" asks Jake Dunleavy.

Jake is a seventh grader who carries a backpack completely covered with buttons that say things like "math is cool" and "ask me the cube root of 2,744." Math *is* cool—at least I think it is but buttons talking about math are not. And lots of people know the cube root of 2,744 is 14.

"He wasn't just *on* Super Quiz Masters Junior." Mr. Dooley again. "He was the champion. Spencer beat out twenty-six other competitors over five days to win the title. He is the reigning Junior Super Quiz Master."

Whoa.

"So you're like famous?" Shelby asks. And giggles.

Spencer was on TV. National TV. For five days in a row. And he won. So yeah, I'd say that makes him sort of famous. And for St. Jude, something like that would make him really famous. A lot more famous than Mary Frances Gonzales and her super summer reading record. Which might be why her face says she'd like to squash him like a bug.

Everyone starts asking Spencer questions about the show. Maya wants to know how hard the questions were. Cameron asks how much money he won. But that's not all he wants to know.

"So Spencer's like a super genius then, right?" But Cameron doesn't wait for an answer. "This'll be good. We'll get to see a real genius in action, not just a barely genius like Gabe."

Every time I start to forget how it felt to punch Cameron in the nose, he says something that makes me want to do it all over again.

"Okay, everyone. I'm sure Mr. Dooley has some very important work to get back to." Sister Stevie walks him to the door and closes it behind him. "Now, we were talking about how math and art can—and do—go together."

"How?" Maya again.

"There are all kinds of math in art," says Spencer. "The best art, anyway. Like the golden ratio and Pascal's triangle. Fibonacci numbers—well, lots of those are in nature but that's kind of art, too. And origami and fractals. Oh, and tessellations. Those are my favorite." The little kid finally runs out of air.

"That's impressive, Spencer. And it's also most of what I'm going to cover over the next few weeks. I hope you'll learn some new things. That you'll all learn some things. New ways of looking at things."

Math and art together. That just seems weird. Of course I'm really good at math. And not exactly really good at art. I kind of thought you couldn't do both. The size of Sister Stevie's smile gives me a clue that I'm going to find out. And that I'm probably going to be wrong. Again.

The bell rings at the same time Sister Stevie says, "Can all my eighth graders stay back for a minute, please?"

The six of us stay in our seats until everyone else gathers up their stuff and races or shuffles out the door.

"Are we going to be late for our next class? I have a test," says Maya.

"This will be quick." Sister starts handing out papers— one for each of us. "Service Hours" is spelled out across the top in giant letters.

Ugh. I totally forgot. At St. Jude, eighth grade means service hours. One more thing to think about.

"Mrs. Capistrano asked me to manage the service hours' requirement for any eighth graders I have this year. And since you're here with me now, I thought this was the perfect time to talk about it."

"What are service hours?" asks Shelby.

I flip through the pages while Sister Stevie talks. Before we graduate, each St. Jude eighth grader has to complete twenty service hours—ten for each semester. We can do just about anything, like babysitting (no way) or raking leaves (maybe) or even helping an old person with things around the house. There's also tutoring, which might be okay.

"I recommend that you think about your talents and how you might best use them in service of others. Pray about it and have some suggestions for me next week."

Maya clears her throat. Loudly.

"And yes, Maya, you may go now." Sister smiles. "Good luck on your test."

Five

"It would be crazy-cool to be famous." Linc's Spanish book slips off his lap and lands on my bedroom floor. Thunk.

"I guess so."

"I mean, I know I couldn't win Super Quiz Masters Junior."

"No kidding."

Linc grabs the pillow off my bed and flings it at my head. Direct hit.

"But I bet I could be famous at something."

"Like?"

"Okay, I don't know. But there has to be something." Linc stares up at the ceiling and taps a beat on his knee. "How old is that Spencer kid, anyway?"

"Maya said he's almost ten. He skipped a couple grades."

"A couple?"

"That's what she said." And if Maya says something, it's true. She's like the CIA or something. Interrogation is one of her specialties.

"I bet that feels weird, huh?" Linc moves on to picking at a scab on his elbow.

"Maybe." What I think is that it probably feels lonely. Spencer uses big words and talks a lot in G.A.S. class, but when I saw him walking down the hallway later, he looked like a scared little kid. Which I guess he is.

"How about if you're famous for passing a Spanish test?"

"Ha ha." But he picks the book back up off the floor and starts reading through the chapter again.

After a few minutes, Linc closes the book, screws his eyes shut tight, and says, *"Me comí el papel higiénico con un pollo."*

"What?"

"Me comí el papel higiénico con un pollo."

"What do you think you said?" I ask.

"I ate a chicken sandwich for lunch." Linc flops onto his back. "That's not what I said?"

"Not quite."

"Then what did I say?"

"I ate toilet paper with a chicken."

We crack up. Then Linc stops and groans.

"I've got to get this. I need an A on this test. An A, Gabe."

"Okay. You'll get it. Try again."

"Hey, when's Maya coming, anyway?"

"She said she's giving us an hour head start since she doesn't need the practice."

Since Mrs. Iing is from Mexico and speaks Spanish around the house, Maya's pretty much totally fluent. And, in the words of our Spanish teacher Señor Dunleavy, her accent is "perfection." Of course it is. I can read Spanish just fine and write it even better, but when I try to speak it something weird happens in my mouth. Señor Dunleavy has a word for my accent, too. And it's not "perfection." Linc's is even worse.

Linc doesn't answer. And he still doesn't answer when I ask him to give me the sentence again. Right, this time. Since he's lying on the floor on the opposite side of my bed, I can't see what he's doing.

"Dude, is this The Flog?" Linc holds up a notebook. A notebook that looks like any of my other school notebooks. A notebook that until just now was hidden under my bed.

"What?"

"It is. The Flog is back." Linc starts flipping through the pages.

"I told you not to call it that."

"I'm sorry. The Gas Gauge then." More flipping. When Linc gets to the pages where the ink is still kind of fresh, he stops. "It's happening again?"

"Haven't you noticed?"

"Maybe a little. But everybody farts. I fart a lot, too."

"Not like this."

"I know. For you it's a *medical condition*." Linc uses his doctor voice—the one that he thinks sounds like his dad but actually sounds exactly like his mom. "But I still don't get how keeping a fart log helps."

I sigh—hugely. "I already explained it to you—twice."

"Yeah, but that was last year. The only thing I remember was coming up with names for different kinds of farts." He flips to the back of the notebook and, after about ten seconds of actually shutting up, Linc starts to chuckle softly. At first.

"Chair Air—remember that one?" More laughter—from Linc. "Those are the ones that come out with such force your butt lifts right off your chair."

"Uh huh."

"Then there was the collection of musical farts—the

trombone, the trumpet, and the tuba." Now he's snorting. "It's like a butt band." And here come the tears. Linc is laughing so hard, he's crying.

"This isn't a joke, you know."

"I know it's not. But it *is* funny." Linc comes and flops down next to me. He waits until the last bits of laughter are gone. Mostly. "Sorry."

"It's all right." And it kind of is. I get that it's funny to Linc. If it was happening to someone else—anyone else—I'd probably think it was funny, too. And even though I don't admit it to Linc, the "butt band" was a good one. Different instruments for different tones. It's actually kind of brilliant.

"So what are you doing about it this time?" Linc asks.

"Well, last year I focused a lot on what I ate."

"So, no beans? Everybody knows beans make you fart."

"Right. Beans totally make you fart. It's the types of sugars in them—people just can't digest them, so they come out as gas. Scientists call those sugars the flatulence factors."

I try to keep a straight face to see if Linc can keep from laughing. He can't. Neither can I. Linc's right—some of this *is* kind of funny.

"But bean farts are all noise and no stink," I say.

"Really?"

"Yep. It's the ones that come from food with lots of sulfur in them that are the real stinkers. Cauliflower, eggs and meat are the worst."

"Huh." Linc sits and thinks for a while. He's scratching away at his pit, which always means he's thinking really hard.

Linc takes my notebook and flips through it some more. There are pages of data—what I ate, when I ate it, whether or not I had stomach cramps, if I had gas. Then if I had gas, there's a table that records the number of farts, the potency of odor, and the volume (how loud, not how many). If it wasn't *my* totally embarrassing problem being analyzed, I'd actually be kind of proud of my research. But it is.

"So what are you doing this time?"

"This time I'm focusing on *how* I eat. And trying to stay relaxed. Eating too fast or chewing gum can make you swallow too much air. That leads to gas. So does being nervous."

"I have a question."

But I'm done talking about farts and The Flog. I know one thing that'll finish Linc off.

"Yes, you should be glad you're not a crinoid."

"A what?"

"A crinoid."

"Okay, why should I be glad I'm not a crinoid? And what is a crinoid, anyway?" he asks.

"It's a marine animal whose anus is right next to its mouth."

And just like I knew it would, the word "anus" sends Linc into hysterics. Rolling on the floor, gut-clutching hysterics. In the middle of all the noise, there's a knock on my door. A loud, hard knock that makes me think it might not have been the first one.

"Come in." I have to yell to be louder than Linc's laughter.

The door swings open and there stands Maya.

"What's so funny?" she asks.

I grab The Flog and whip it back under my bed, then whack Linc in the arm to get him to shut up. It doesn't work. When he's this far gone, nothing works.

"Um, nothing," I say.

She looks from me to Linc and back again. Then she raises her left eyebrow. I used to think she was reading my mind when she did that. Sometimes I still do.

This time Maya lets us off the hook. Sort of.

"Linc ríe como un loco." I translate that easlly—Linc laughs like a lunatic.

"Sí." Yep.

After Linc and Maya left it was homework, dinner, and now more homework. Just like every other day since school started. My brain feels even fuller than my stomach, and I had three helpings of spaghetti and meatballs for dinner plus two pieces of apple pie.

When the knock on my door comes, I'm hanging off either side of my bed trying to make some room in both my brain and my stomach.

"Come in."

"Hi, sweetheart." It's my grandma. She came for dinner tonight. She does that sometimes now—comes for dinner in the middle of the week. And she always brings pie. "May I come all the way in?"

"Sure." I pull myself up and make room for her to sit down.

"So, tomorrow . . ." Grandma's voice trails off.

My dad talked about our upcoming CSMHS visit all during dinner. I guess Grandma thinks there's more to say. I don't.

Grandma takes a giant breath in and says, "I'm going golfing."

"What?"

"Yep. Tomorrow. 8:45 tee time—just like it always was."

Just like it always was.

"Oh."

"It's the first time I'm going to golf without him. We golfed together for forty-seven years, you know." Grandma twists her wedding ring around and around on her finger.

I don't know what to say. When I think about my grandpa—which is a lot—I think about how sad I am that he died and how much I miss him. I guess I forget to think about how much my grandma misses him.

"I'm probably going to be rusty. And I'm sure I'll be able to hear Grandpa telling me to take my time, not to hurry my swing." She laughs one of those shaky laughs that has tears mixed in. "I probably still won't listen."

"He knows you won't." I grin and we both laugh. A real one this time.

"It's hard to do things without Grandpa that I always thought I'd do with him, you know?" she says.

"I know."

I play with a loose thread on my bedspread, pulling and pulling until it's so long I've probably unraveled something important. When I look up, Grandma's eyes are like lasers, staring straight through me to the back of my brain. My dad tells me that when he was a kid he could never keep anything from Grandma. She had secret powers or something that made people tell her things. She still does.

"So, Carolina Science and Math High School." The words leave her mouth and seem to land with a plop in the middle of my bed. I can feel them sitting there, waiting for something from me.

I don't want to talk about it. It feels too big to talk about. But Grandma's eyes stay on me until it comes out in a rush anyway. "It was a me-and-Grandpa thing, you know? And I'm not sure I can do it without him."

"But *I* know you can. And Grandpa knows that, too."

Grandma reaches out and taps the Saint Gabriel medal that hangs around my neck. The one that was Grandpa's. "I know I'm not him. And I won't try to be. But I'm here. And I'll be rooting for you just as hard as he would."

She stands up and leans over to kiss the top of my head. Then my grandma, who runs marathons and never does anything softly or quietly, slips out the door and eases it shut behind her. It closes without making a sound.

I flop back onto my back and watch Celsius and Fahrenheit swim around and around in their fishbowl.

Glug.

Six

"There was a misprint on the lunch menu."

Mrs. Vincent, the lunch lady, says it like it's no big deal. Like having someone slop a giant ladleful of goulash onto your tray when you were expecting tacos isn't a tragedy. It is. The goulash doesn't look good and it sure doesn't smell good either. They say it's just noodles and meat and vegetables mixed together. But it's all smothered in some kind of red sauce—there could be anything in there.

On my way to our table, I pass Maya and Shelby. Except for the part of last year where she wasn't speaking to me, Maya always ate lunch with Linc and me. At our table. But ever since the first day of school, she sits with Shelby.

"Hey," I say.

The "hey" starts out regular but turns into kind of a question. Because Maya looks different. Instead of hanging in her eyes like always, her bangs are pulled to the side with some kind of clip. A sparkly clip. And her lips are pink and shiny.

Maya takes a nibble of her sandwich and waves some new kind of wave that only uses the tips of her fingers. Shelby giggles. Of course.

Once I finally wind my way through and around the crowd of eighth graders that stand between me and our table, I plunk my tray down and start talking. "Have you noticed anything different about Maya?"

Linc smirks. "Maya's a girl, right?"

Of course. Linc notices everything about any girl within a seven-mile radius. So even if it's only Maya, and Linc says she doesn't technically qualify as a "girl-girl" since she's been our friend since forever, he'd still notice.

"Okay, so what does it all mean? The lip gloss and the new hair and other stuff."

"What other stuff?" Linc devours half his sandwich in one bite.

"Well, she smells like strawberries all the time. She

never used to smell like strawberries. Is it the lip gloss? Is it strawberry flavored or something?"

"Yes, it's the lip gloss. Most girl lip gloss is fruit flavored. That or bubble gum." Linc swallows another giant bite of sandwich. "I can't believe you're the one with the sister. Why do I know so much more about girls?"

I ignore him and ask the question I really need an answer to. "She keeps looking at me sideways. It's like she has a stiff neck and can't turn her head or something."

"Meaningful glances," says Linc.

"What are you talking about?"

"Those are called 'meaningful glances.' I thought everyone knew that."

"Everyone who reads your mom's romance novels maybe, but not me."

Linc kicks me under the table and looks around to make sure no one heard.

"Sorry."

I'm not really sorry. Reading your mom's romance novels is a reason to get made fun of. It just is. But I don't want to get kicked again, plus I need more information.

"So if these glances are supposed to be meaningful, then what do they mean?"

Linc slurps the last drops of milk in his carton. "Nobody knows."

"What do you mean nobody knows?" This conversation is more confusing than Maya's new hair and sideways-looking problem.

"I mean that nobody really knows. No guy, anyway."

I look down at my lunch, the lunch I haven't touched. The goulash looks even worse now than it did in line. The sauce has a weird shine that makes it look slippery. Food should never look slippery. I scoop up a forkful anyway. But when the bite is halfway to my mouth, something or someone thumps my shoulder and the bite of goulash catapults off my fork. Linc dodges to the left just in time to avoid it.

"Nice reflexes," says Jack McGinnis, one of the guys on last year's basketball team and the source of the shoulder thumping. He fist bumps Linc and slides into the seat next to me like that's where he sits every day. It's not.

"Hey, Gabe."

"Hey."

Flick Phillips, another basketball player, sits down next to Linc, grunts at me, and shoves six french fries into his mouth.

Linc's smile takes up more than half his face. "There's an informational meeting about tryouts after school today and the guys said they'd tell me what's going to happen."

"Okay." Linc's parents haven't said yes about basketball yet. But they haven't said no either. Tryouts start in two weeks, so if Linc's going to get a "yes," he needs it soon.

While Linc is finding out all there is to know about basketball tryouts, I'll be at CSMHS with my dad. We're going on a tour and then meeting with a counselor or teacher or something. And right now was when I was going to tell Linc about it. About not being here this afternoon and about maybe not being at Catholic Central with him next year.

I was going to tell him. But then Maya changed her hair and put on lip gloss and looked at me sideways and I needed to ask Linc about all that. And then Jack and Flick showed up.

Basketball talk swirls around me while I again contemplate what's on my tray. My stomach is sending clear and loud signals that it would like to be fed. My brain tells it to take a good look at what's coming. My stomach is louder.

I breathe through my mouth. Science says if I can't smell the goulash, I won't taste it either. I shovel a few forkfuls into my mouth and wash it down with two chocolate milks. Science forgot to consider the power of the aftertaste. Ugh.

Even though there are fifteen minutes left for lunch, I stand up. "I'm going to the library."

"Okay. See you later," says Linc.

"Actually, no. I'm leaving after next period. I have an appointment."

Linc's already back to talking jump shots with Jack.

"And this is the Hall of Labs." Dr. Tremaine is one of the assistant principals and our tour guide. We stroll past door after door as Dr. Tremaine describes what's inside—labs for chemistry, physics, and biology are first. Then it's on to the engineering and robotics labs.

"Whoa." I don't know I'm going to say it out loud until after it's out there.

"Exactly." Dr. Tremaine's smile splits his face in two.

"Is there anything for meteorology? Because Gabe is really interested in the weather," says my dad.

"Well, yes. There's a one-semester elective that you can take your sophomore or junior year. And there's a meteorology club that meets Tuesdays during lunch."

"How many members are there?" I ask.

"Twenty-six. I'm actually the faculty advisor. We do a lot of really interesting experiments and studies." There's the giant grin again. "It's pretty awesome."

It sounds pretty awesome. And twenty-six members? That's twenty-four and a half more members than my old club had (Linc only counted as a half since he never participated in the discussions).

"And of course with your win in the Academic Olympics last year, you'd have a good chance of making our team," says Dr. Tremaine. "It's a pretty big deal around here."

He comes to a halt in front of an enormous trophy case—it's at least four times bigger than the one at St. Jude. And instead of being chock full of football and basketball trophies like ours is, the trophies inside this case have microscopes and globes and DNA strings on them. One even has a crystal octahedron balanced on the point of one of its eight triangular sides. Again—whoa.

My dad cranes his neck and searches around the trophy case. I know what he's looking for. "So, how about sports? I don't see many sports trophies."

"Actually, down here on the end we have an impressive display of awards our crew and cross country teams have won."

Impressive? I count four trophies—and they're all kind of small.

"But no basketball, huh? Or football?"

"We don't have a football team, Mr. Carpenter." My dad flinches like someone just sucker punched him. "As for our basketball team . . . ," Dr. Tremaine pauses and scratches his chin. "They always give it their best effort."

I know and I know my dad knows that's code for "they stink." My dad flinches a second time. He stares at Dr. Tremaine for a minute and then nods his head. "Okay. Well, what's next?"

What's next is us hanging out in the back of a trigonometry class for the last seventeen minutes of class. Even though I don't understand a lot of it, my fingers itch to grab a pencil and try to follow along. When the bell rings, the kids rush for the door, pushing and shoving a little just like at St. Jude. Like regular kids. Which I guess they are. Regular kids who happen to like science and math a whole lot. Just like me.

There's a lot more talking—by Dr. Tremaine—and a lot more questions—from my dad. I'm mostly quiet. We get to the door and I push through. Outside. Some leaves from the big oak on the front lawn have fallen and swirl around in the breeze. I watch them while I wait for the talking to stop. I keep my eyes trained on those leaves dancing just above the ground. Not looking up. Not looking at the sky.

I tune back in long enough to hear Dr. Tremaine tell my dad about the process—the application and teacher recommendations, the test and the interview.

"So how many of the kids who apply actually get in?" my dad asks. Which is pretty much exactly what I was wondering.

"Our average acceptance rate is 28.75 percent."

That means that only one out of every 3.48 applicants gets in. I don't know what 0.48 of a kid looks like, but math doesn't lie.

I might not get in.

That thought winds its way to a place near the back of my brain and settles in to be examined later.

We finally say goodbye to Dr. Tremaine. He gives me a CSMHS T-shirt (it's navy blue and has the Pythagorean theorem on the front and the periodic table on the back). Then he tells me—three times—how much he enjoyed meeting me and how much he would enjoy having me as a student next year. I guess *he* thinks I'd get in. I shake his hand, which is soft and squishy, and mumble a thank you. My dad shakes his hand hard enough that Dr. Tremaine lets out a tiny squeak.

I start counting. It takes fourteen seconds for my dad to ask.

"So? Was that incredible or what?" He slugs me in the arm. My dad is a lot like the football players at school. He's always jostling me with his shoulder or slugging me in the arm or clapping me on the back.

"Yeah. It was really cool."

"What do you think?" he asks.

"I think I'm hungry." Actually my stomach is clenching so badly I'm not sure I could eat anything, but food is a good way to change the subject with my dad.

"Me, too. Barbecue?" I nod. "Chet's?" I nod again.

We get all the way to the car before I forget not to look up. And there it is. The heaven sky. Altostratus clouds cover most of the sky. They block most of the sun. But not all. Some rays shine through. It's the sky that always makes me think of heaven. And Grandpa.

I guess I knew he'd find a way to be here today.

Two guys, four pulled-pork sandwiches, and a pile of onion rings so high I have to use perfectly straight church posture to see my dad over them.

My dad is still talking. "And those labs. I couldn't believe all of those labs. That physiology lab was cooler than the one we had in college." A blob of coleslaw slips out from under the bun on my dad's sandwich and falls onto his plate. He uses an onion ring to scoop it up and pops the whole thing into his mouth. My dad calls himself a virtuoso of western-style North Carolina barbecue. A pulled-pork expert. He might be right.

"They were pretty cool." They were more than cool. The word I kept thinking over and over was the same one my dad said. Incredible.

"So your mom told me not to pester you too much, but she's not here." My dad grins.

No kidding she's not here. If she was, there wouldn't be so much chomping and slurping and talking with our mouths full.

"That place seemed just right for you, Champ."

"Yeah."

"I know it's kind of far from home."

"Fifty-seven-minute bus ride each way. More if traffic is bad." I know all this already.

"Right. And that's on top of a longer school day. It might not leave time for much else."

Much else like climbing trees with Maya and playing H-I-P-P-O-P-O-T-A-M-U-S with Linc in the driveway and sneaking Mom's cookies right after school.

"You don't think I should go? I mean if I even get in." Is it because there's no football?

My dad guzzles the rest of his sweet tea and sits back in his seat.

"No, that's not at all what I think."

My dad pays the bill and we walk out to the car. He waits until we're on the highway heading toward home to answer the question I didn't ask.

"I was watching you and I saw your face. You loved it."
He turns the radio to some sports talk show. Two guys
are discussing college football, talking over each other in
voices that get louder and louder.

"Yeah. I did." There's no way my dad heard me over
the sound of the two guys yelling at each other about
which quarterback should start Sunday's game. Still, he
reaches over and ruffles my hair.

When we get home, I sit on my bed and stare at the
still-blank application. And then I take a deep breath,
pick up my pen, and write my name at the top. I buzz
through the first few questions. Name, address, phone
number, birthdate are all a slam dunk. But when I get to
extra-curricular activities, my pen skitters to a halt.

There are five lines.

For five *different* activities.

I can't exactly put the weather club down. I mean,
we only met three times and nothing actually happened
other than Linc complaining about the cookies I brought.
My mom was on a raisin kick then and Linc hates raisins.
So no actual weather club kind of stuff happened.

I fill in the Academic Olympics. That was a big deal.
We won and all. And I was a co-captain. So that shows

leadership, right? And leadership is good. But still, it's only one line. The other four lines stare at me all white and blank and accusing. Something tells me—the something that's usually right about things—the one kid out of 3.48 who gets accepted to CSMHS has more than a single line filled in. And if I want to be that kid, I'm going to need more than one line, too.

Seven

Maybe it's because my dad and I got home pretty late last night. Or maybe it's because my brain keeps going back to yesterday—the tour, the trophies, the T-shirt, the blank lines on my application. Whatever the reason, this day has been one big mess-up. I brought the wrong notebook to first period, the wrong book to third, and was late for history because I started walking in the opposite direction and didn't figure it out until the bell rang. I even forgot my lunch money and had to walk home for lunch. The best thing about today is that it's almost over.

I sneak into Saint Jude's corner on my way to religion class. He's just standing there (he's a statue, so that's pretty much the only move he's got) looking like he knows things. Part of me is convinced that he's just a statue. The other part of me thinks he's here to watch over us and that he has the answers. That he just hangs out in here all day watching us kids mess things up over and over again, waiting for us to ask for his help. Last year I did. And it worked. So I'm back.

A guy wouldn't want to be caught having an actual conversation with a statue, so I go with the old need-to-tie-my-shoe move. I crouch down next to Saint Jude and half pray, half talk silently. Sometime during the praying and the talking, my insides start to unknot. And right before the one-minute warning bell rings, I throw in a little request to make me taller. Just in case that isn't a total lost cause after all.

The squeak of bike brakes tells me I'm not alone anymore. The particular pitch of the squeak tells me who it is without having to turn around.

"Hey."

"Yeah, hey." I keep drawing circles in the dirt with a stick, each one smaller than the last.

Maya sits on the ground next to me but not right next to me. Before last year, she would have sat right next to me, her knee touching mine. But now there's always a space between us, almost wide enough for a whole other person. It's like the space knows that last year Maya said some things and I might have—or might not have—felt some things. But we both ignored all the things and now there's just the space. Sometimes I barely notice it, but other times it seems miles wide.

"Are you going?" she asks.

"Where?"

"Gabe, come on." Maya blows her bangs up out of her eyes and rests her chin on her knees.

"How did you know?" Because I didn't tell her yet. Or Linc. I didn't tell anybody yet.

"I'm a woman. I know everything." She snorts. "Actually, your mom told my mom when she dropped cookies off at the bookstore after school. I wasn't supposed to be listening. Your mom's worried about you. She says you're not saying much. My mom thinks you'll be fine. They both think you should go."

"So."

"So, are you going to go?"

"I don't know. I might not even get in," I say. I scribble 1/3.48 in the dirt. Then 28.75%.

Maya rolls her eyes. Twice. "Right. They made that school just for science and math geniuses like you."

I shrug and grunt something that's not a word, then go back to drawing circles in the dirt.

"How about you?" I ask. "You'd totally get in. So why don't you want to go?"

Maya watches a butterfly flit from the tip of one weed to the next before it flies away. "I'm too much of a renaissance woman."

"What?"

"Carolina Science and Math High School. I mean, it's right there in the name. It's all about science and math. But I love music, too. And languages. I'm going to learn Mandarin. Well, more Mandarin, anyway. My dad's pretty geeked about that. And writing. I want to work on my writing. I want to do it all."

"So Catholic Central for you?"

"Yep."

There it is. If I go to CSMHS, it'll be just me. No matter how incredible it all is, it would be just me. No Linc. And no Maya.

"You know you'd be crazy not to go." Maya's voice is so sure.

"Maybe." My voice is the opposite of sure.

I finish drawing the smallest circle and toss the stick aside.

"Want to climb the tree?" asks Maya. The tree is the enormous red oak we've been climbing since we were old enough to reach the lowest branches.

"Okay."

Maya still climbs trees. Even if some stuff is weird and confusing, she still climbs trees.

We don't say anything else until we step across what would be a creek any other time of the year. Since today's the last day of summer—by the calendar anyway, even though we've been in school for thirty-one days—the creek bed is completely dry, full of cracks and crevices.

"You want to go first?" It's a stupid question, really. Maya always goes first. Plus she already has a grip on the first branch and is about to swing her lead leg up.

She climbs as high as she always climbs, which is two branches higher than I always climb. I settle into my spot—there's this joint in the tree where two thick branches meet the trunk. I lean back into it and peer up through the leaves at Maya, then past her to the sky. Cumulus clouds today. Fair weather, but moving fast.

Eight

Open Gym means open for everyone, right? Not just kids who are going to actually play something. But someone like me who's got data to gather, numbers to crunch, and results to analyze. Open Gym is for guys like that, too; I'm almost sure. But still, in case that's not what they mean, I pick a spot up high in the bleachers. A spot tucked away in one of the corners where I can still see everything clearly, but it's easy not to notice me. So far it's worked. Other than Linc, who I came with, and my dad, who dropped us off, nobody seems to know—or care—that I'm here.

Sunday night Open Gym always has chaperones. Tonight it's Coach Schwimmer and Mr. Nicholls, the other gym teacher. They're sprawled across the bottom two rows of bleachers closest to the door—as far from me as they could be.

My tools surround me. Two notebooks, four pencils, three pieces of graph paper, and a ruler. A calculator makes a bulge in the pocket of my shorts, but that's just in case I need to double check my own calculations.

Linc's part of the four-on-four game going on. It's him and a bunch of guys who are going to try out for the team. Tryouts start one week from tomorrow. And Linc still hasn't gotten a "yes" from his parents. He hasn't gotten a "no," either. His grades have been better than ever. Almost perfect, in fact. But I still think it could go either way.

"Whooooop!" Linc gets another rebound, dribbles the length of the court, and sinks a sweet jumper. His game is on tonight. He turns and gives me a long-distance high five. I send one right back. Unfortunately, all the high fiving alert Coach Schwimmer and Mr. Nicholls to my position. They both turn and look up to where I'm perched. Mr. Nicholls turns right back around. Coach Schwimmer studies me long enough for Linc's team to get the ball back and score again. Then he unfolds himself from the bleachers and starts climbing.

Boom. Boom. Boom.

Each step echoes through the gym.

Boom. Boom. Boom.

Each boom brings him closer to me.

I put my head down and work out some quick calculations—offensive versus defensive rebounds.

Coach climbs to the top bleacher—the one I'm sitting on—and leans back against the wall. I stick with the whole pretend-you-don't-know-he's-there move.

"So, granny shots. That was you, huh?"

"Yes, sir."

He does remember who I am. And not just because of the whole rope-climbing thing. Linc says it qualifies as an "incident," but I still say it was more of a mishap.

Part of seventh grade phys ed—a really horrible part—is that they make you climb up a thick rope that has knots tied In It. The rope is attached to the ceiling so it's not like you're even trying to climb *to* anywhere.

When it was my turn, I got past the first knot. And the second. But then I slipped. And fell. Onto Coach Schwimmer's foot. I was okay, but his left hallux wasn't. Yeah, I broke his big toe.

"Not playing tonight?"

"No, sir."

He nudges one of my notebooks with his enormous shoe. The left one. "Homework?"

"Not exactly." I nod toward the court where Flick shoots—and misses—a three-pointer. I make two notations in one notebook. Result: missed shot. Cause: radio-ulnar deviation. Also known as not keeping the wrist in the neutral position. "It's that." Linc snags the rebound and lobs a pass far ahead to Jack, who scores an easy layup. "And all that." That's three separate notations in three different spots.

"You're keeping stats?" Coach asks. His voice sounds more interested than it did a minute ago.

"Keeping them and analyzing them."

"Analyzing them how?"

I hand him one of the pieces of graph paper. It's the one that compares offensive and defensive rebounds for each of the guys who's playing.

Coach makes one of those grunting noises that could mean he thought my graph was interesting. Or it could mean he's thinking about turning it into a paper airplane and seeing how far it'll fly.

This isn't how this was supposed to go. I had plans. Plans that looked like me going to Coach's office and presenting my findings with reports and color-coded charts. But it looks like it's going to be now. Me and Coach Schwimmer on the bleachers.

"I was thinking that maybe you could use someone like me on the team."

"You want to try out for the team?" Coach Schwimmer doesn't even try not to sound surprised.

"Oh, no. I stink at actually playing basketball." He doesn't disagree. "I mean use me doing this. Keeping stats for all the players and maybe figuring some stuff out."

Coach doesn't say anything, but he does sit down. He flips through each of my notebooks, page by page. He grabs a pencil and makes some calculations of his own—checking my work, I guess. When he's done, he goes back to the rebound graph.

"So we've got a couple guys who're a little lazy on defense, huh?" he says.

"That's one conclusion," I say.

"What's another?"

"Well, Flick likes to stay at the top of the key when he's on defense. So he doesn't get as many chances at defensive rebounds. But he's a killer on the other end." I point out Flick's offensive rebound numbers. They're good.

"How would I know that from looking at your graph?" asks Coach.

I turn the paper over. "That's where the commentary comes in. I take notes that go along with the graphs. You can't just look at numbers."

Coach nods.

"So you're looking for a job?" he asks.

"Sort of," I say. "I mean, you don't have to pay me or anything. It'd just be like I was part of the team."

Nothing. No nod. No words. Nothing. And since Coach doesn't say anything, neither do I. We sit, side-by-sort-of-side, and watch the game. Linc shoots a three-pointer—swish. He's so pumped he turns a cartwheel on the way back up the court. Coach chuckles and finally turns to me.

"How about a trial run?" he says.

"Sir?"

Coach nods a few times and stands up. I can almost see the idea working around in his head. "Yeah, a trial run. You'll do this during tryouts and then we'll go from there."

"Um, okay." I still don't know if I got the job or didn't get the job.

"I mean you'll come to tryouts and do all of this." He gestures toward my notes and graphs. "Then after we figure out who makes the team, you and I can sit down and figure out if there's a spot for you."

Coach starts his way down the bleachers. Boom. Boom. Boom.

"Um, okay."

Boom. Boom. Boom.

All the air leaves my lungs. And my intestines.

I'm going to be part of the team. During tryouts, anyway. And I know that when Coach sees what I can do, I'll have a job for the rest of the season. I just know it.

For a minute, I think about doing a cartwheel of my own.

Nine

"I'm anxious to hear what you've all chosen."

Sister Stevie opens an official-looking binder labeled "Eighth Grade Service Hours." She has a separate tab for each of us.

"So, who's first?"

I wait for Maya to go first. Maya always goes first. But she doesn't say anything. And when I look over at her, she doesn't look like she's going to say anything. She's busy chewing the gloss off her lower lip and trying to recapture the hunk of bangs that escaped her hair clip.

No one else says anything either. Sister's smile starts to slip.

"Tutoring," I say. "I'll pick tutoring."

The smile comes back, bigger than before.

"That's wonderful, Gabe. Just wonderful."

"Me, too." It's Maya's voice. But Maya's not a "me, too" person. She's a "me, first" person. She always has been.

Weird.

Again.

Linc picks yard work. He told me he was going to because he thinks it's going to be easy. I didn't say anything, but since Linc's family uses a landscaping service and he's never even pulled a weed, I'm not sure it's going to be as easy as he thinks.

Cameron picks recycling. That actually does sound easy.

It's finally Shelby's turn. And without swinging her hair or giggling even once, she chooses babysitting. She says her neighbor is really sick and needs help with her kids.

"That sounds wonderful, Shelby," says Sister Stevie. "I'm sure she'll really appreciate the help."

Sister Stevie finishes writing down everyone's choices in her big binder.

"Please remember to have your forms filled out and signed by a supervising adult," Sister Stevie says. "Gabe and Maya, please stay for another minute. The rest of you can go."

"The two of you will be working with fourth graders at St. Jude Elementary," says Sister Stevie. "Tomorrow after school, you'll go over and meet with Mrs. Winnegan. She'll tell you all about your students and how you'll be helping them. She'll also answer any questions you have."

Mrs. Winnegan was my fourth grade teacher. She was really nice and always made stuff fun when it could have been boring. Like when we had to learn all fifty state capitals, she made up songs and games. That's why I still know that Pierre is the capital of South Dakota and that Pennsylvania's capital is Harrisburg even though pretty much everybody always thinks it's Philadephia.

Maya asks a bunch of questions even though Sister Stevie just said Mrs. Winnegan would tell us everything. Sister doesn't have those answers, but she does talk—for a long time—about how wonderful this will be for us and for the students. And how we shouldn't be nervous because the teachers will tell us what to do and—if we get stuck—we should listen for the Holy Spirit to guide us.

I wasn't nervous before now. I mean, I tutored Becca and other than the whole "she's my sister's best friend and I had a huge crush on her and asked her out and she said no and my sister hated me even more than usual" part, it was a success. Becca's math grade got a lot better. I even made enough money to buy an architectural LEGO set I'd been wanting forever—the Akashi-Kaikyo Bridge in Japan. It's the longest suspension bridge in the world, and building it took forever and made me even more sure I want to be a civil engineer. If I'm not a meteorologist. So yeah, last time tutoring was pretty good. But if Sister Stevie thinks we'll need the Holy Spirit's help, maybe this time it won't be so easy.

I find the guidance counselor's office where Mrs. Winnegan asked me to meet her and knock on the door. Mrs. Winnegan opens it.

"Gabe!" She hugs me and then steps back to really look at me. "Look at you. You're so tall and handsome." I'm not, but she really seems to mean it so I just smile.

"I'm so glad you've decided to volunteer. I have someone I'm sure you can help," she says.

"Okay."

"His name is Harry. Harry Newton. And he's a fourth grader—he's nine years old."

"Okay."

"Harry is really smart, like you." I start to ask why he needs a tutor if he's so smart, but Mrs. Winnegan isn't finished. "Harry also has some challenges. He has

ADHD—Attention Deficit Hyperactivity Disorder. Do you know what that is?"

"Kind of. I mean, I've heard of it and I know some kids who have it, but I don't think I know what it really means," I say.

"No problem. For Harry, it means that he has trouble concentrating. It's difficult for him to focus and stay organized. He needs to be taught some things more than once," Mrs. Winnegan pauses and focuses on the space somewhere over my head. "Sometimes a lot more than once. And he's a wonderful boy, but friendships can be hard for him."

"Oh." I have a lot of questions. But the only one I ask is, "What do you want me to do?"

"Harry has a team of people who help him here and outside of school. You'll be like a junior member of that team. To start, I'm going to have you practice spelling with Harry."

"Okay." I hope I don't sound as clueless as I feel. Mrs. Winnegan might fire me before I even meet Harry.

"I'm going to let you go meet Harry on your own first. He's waiting in my classroom," she says. "And don't worry. You'll do great."

As I walk down the hall trying to remember all that Mrs. Winnegan just told me, I remember Sister Stevie telling us to ask the Holy Spirit for help. Now I know why.

"Your head's not much bigger than a regular person's head."

"What?"

"I said your head isn't really any bigger than a regular person's." A skinny kid sits cross-legged on top of a desk in the corner of the room scratching his head with a pencil. He's the only person in the room.

"Are you Harry?" I ask.

"Yeah." The scratching stops, but now he's using the pencil to drum out a beat on his knee. "And you're supposed to be a genius. But I figure if you really *are* a genius, your brain must be bigger than a regular person's. And if your brain is bigger, then your head would have to be bigger, too. You know, to hold the extra brain parts. But it's not. Not really, anyway. It's kinda hard to tell though, 'cuz your hair's so poufy."

"My hair's poufy?"

"Like you didn't know." The kid rolls his eyes—he's almost as good at it as Sabrina. "So is it true? Are you a genius? 'Cuz Jimmy Conrad—he lives next door to me—his sister is a seventh grader and Jimmy said that she said that you are." Harry finally stops to take a breath.

I look around for Mrs. Winnegan. I know she said she wanted me to meet Harry on my own, but the meeting part is over. And right now I'd be happy to see her—or anyone—who would make this kid stop talking about my not-so-big head and poufy hair.

"Mrs. Winnegan said she'd be right back. She's my teacher. She's actually pretty nice. I think she had to go to the bathroom. She's been gone for a while." The kid cracks up.

"Okay. Well, maybe we should just wait for her." I sit down at a desk close to the door.

Harry jumps down from his desk and comes over to stand next to me. Right next to me. So close that I can smell the corn chips he must have had for lunch and see the faint remains of a chocolate milk mustache.

"Are you one of those people who doesn't answer questions?"

"No. But I am one of those people who can't answer fourteen questions at the same time."

"Got it." Harry bounces from foot to foot but doesn't say anything else.

"Yeah, I'm supposed to be a genius."

"I knew it."

"But my brain isn't any bigger than anyone else's. I just got a high score on a test and I really like to learn things.

That's all." I reach up and feel the top of my head. "And yes, my hair is poufy. I can't help that either."

He laughs—a loud, cackly kind of laugh—and I can't help but laugh, too. Then Harry's laugh stops mid-cackle and his face goes serious.

"Can I ask you one more question?" he says.

"Sure."

"If you're a genius, does that mean you can fix me?"

Before I can ask Harry what he means, Mrs. Winnegan comes in.

"Gabe, you're here." Mrs. Winnegan acts surprised to see me. I guess she doesn't want Harry to know we were talking about him. "You two have met?"

"Yep."

"Okay. Well then, good." Mrs. Winnegan goes over to her desk. "I thought you two could work on this week's spelling words. How does that sound?"

It sounds pretty easy to me until I glance over at Harry. His foot is tapping about a million miles an hour, but he's just staring out the window. His face is blank like Linc's gets when I talk about barometric pressure.

"Okay," I say. "Where should we work?"

"Well, I have a parent coming to meet with me in a few minutes, so I thought the two of you could work in the courtyard. Just knock on the door if you need anything." Mrs. Winnegan hands me a list of spelling words and another piece of paper.

Courtyard is a fancy name for two concrete benches, one tree, and a couple of scraggly bushes that I think are supposed to have flowers on them. They don't.

I slide onto one of the benches and wait for Harry to stop moving. Harry leaps onto and then almost immediately off of the other bench and then starts pacing back and forth between the tree and one of the sad-looking bushes. His fingers fly as he twirls the same stubby pencil from his thumb down to his pinky and back again. My fingers could never do that.

I notice there are only five words on the paper Mrs. Winnegan gave me. That seems weird—I remember spelling tests from fourth grade and there were more like twenty words every week.

"Okay." I stand in the only sliver of shade I can find and try to stay out of Harry's way. "Spelling words, huh? How about if I just give you a word and you spell it for me?"

"How about if I don't?"

What?

"Um, Mrs. Winnegan said we should work on your spelling words."

Harry says nothing and his eyes stay focused on his fingers.

"Is there another way you want to do this? Do you want to write them down?" I mean, I figured just asking him to spell the words out loud was the way to go, but I could be wrong.

"I can't spell those words."

"How do you know? You haven't tried."

Maybe it's like when my dad was teaching me how to ride a two-wheeler. I was convinced that gravity made it impossible to actually stay upright, balanced on two skinny wheels. Without ever trying, six-year-old—okay, almost seven-year-old—me knew I couldn't do it. I was so sure. But it turned out my dad was right. I did do it. Eventually.

"Okay," I say. "The first word is 'panda.'"

Silence.

It's like Harry turned into a different person when we came outside. In the classroom, he said about a thousand words. But since we came outside, almost nothing.

"Um, the word is 'panda.' You know, like a panda bear." Maybe he's not sure what I said. Or what the word means. Or something.

"Yeah, I know what a panda bear *is*." Harry's hands aren't flying anymore. They're balled into fists at his sides. And he's finally standing still. When he raises his eyes to look at me, they're shiny with tears. "I just can't spell it. Not right now, anyway."

Oh, man. I made him cry. There's no way Mrs. Winnegan is going to sign my service hours sheet if I made a kid cry. On the first day.

"Hey, Harry, I'm really sorry." He shakes his head and chews on his thumbnail. "No, really. I'm supposed to be a genius but there are lots of things I'm really bad at. Like basketball. And girls. And I guess, this."

Harry comes and stands next to me. Too close again. He reaches over and slides the second piece of paper out of my hand. The one I never looked at.

"This is my spelling test."

At first I think he's kidding. But no one has ever looked less like someone playing a joke than Harry looks right now. There are five words written on the page. At least I think they're words. The letters are spiky and hard to read, but the ones I can read don't actually spell anything.

"I had the same words last week. I studied so hard. I knew them—all five of them. I did." Harry shoves his hands deep in his pockets. "I really did."

"I believe you," I say.

"You do?"

"Yeah," I say. "If you say you knew them, then I believe you."

"I did. I totally did. My mom even quizzed me during breakfast and again right when she dropped me off. I knew all five. We were going to go out for ice cream if I got them all right."

Harry starts to pace again—back and forth between the tree and the bush.

"But then there was a fire drill so Mrs. Winnegan didn't give me the test right away like she usually does. And I ripped my piece of paper and had to get a new one. And then Sam had to sharpen his pencil. Right when Mrs. Winnegan gave me the first word."

"What happened?" I cringe, because I already know. The evidence is in my hand.

"I tried so hard to keep all those letters straight in my head. But I could feel them leaking out and getting all mixed up." Harry stops but keeps his head pointed down so I can only see the top of his head. "I got them all wrong. My mom wanted to take me for ice cream anyway, but I said no. I got them all wrong."

Someone else should be here. Someone smarter than me. Someone who knows what to do and what to say. Because I don't. Not even a little bit.

"Okay," I finally say. "Um, how about if we start with the second word?"

While I wait for Linc to show up to play H-I-P-P-O-P-O-T-A-M-U-S, every minute of me trying to help Harry plays over and over in my head like a bad movie. I wonder if it's too late to switch service hours. Landscaping would be better than this—even babysitting might be better. Harry couldn't spell table—the second word on the list—any better than he spelled "panda." He couldn't spell the third, fourth, or fifth words either. Nothing I tried worked. It was a total failure. *I* was a total failure.

I flop back onto the grass and stare up at the sky. The feathery cirrus clouds I noticed earlier today have morphed into round, fluffy looking cirrocumulus. When we were little kids, Sabrina and I thought they were the best clouds for cloud watching. We'd lie on our backs in the yard and make cloud pictures. She never wanted to hear about the science of clouds or what they could tell you. She still doesn't. But clouds can tell you a lot. And sometimes it's not what you'd think. Like these puffy, cotton ball-looking clouds. They mean that sometime before twenty-four hours are up, we're going to have a storm.

Today's the day I'm finally going to tell Linc about applying to CSMHS. I have to tell him. Linc not knowing feels wrong. But my stomach clenches up thinking about what he's going to say. Because even though Maya says I should go—that I've *got* to go—I'm pretty sure Linc is going to say the exact opposite.

The rattle of Linc's unreliable bike chain, which I've told him he needs to fix at least a hundred times, means I hear Linc coming before I see him. He rockets down the street and turns hard into my driveway.

"Gabe, hey Gabe! Guess what?" Linc hits the brakes hard and skids to a stop. Four more inches and he would've run me over.

Linc whips off his helmet and there's an expression on his face I've never seen.

"What's going on?" I ask. "Are you okay?"

"I'm better than okay." Now it looks like he's going to either start dancing or pee his pants. I hope for neither.

"Then what? Just tell me."

"They said yes. My mom and dad. They said yes."

My face must tell Linc I still don't know what he means because he opens his eyes so wide his eyeballs look like they're in danger of popping out.

"Wait, basketball? They said yes to basketball?" I scramble to my feet. This is definitely a standing up conversation.

"Yes. Can you believe it?"

The truth is, I can't. I never really believed that Linc had a chance—or a prayer.

"But how?"

"Mrs. Capistrano. We met with her right after school and after about a million minutes of talking about it, she took my side. Well, kind of. There are conditions—a lot of conditions—and I had to sign a contract. But they said yes. I'm going to be on the basketball team. I mean, if I make it. But I will. I'll make it and then I'll be on the team. The actual team." Linc fake dribbles and takes an imaginary shot. "Swish."

"Wow."

"I know, right? Both of us trying out. We're going to be on the team together. Isn't that awesome?"

Before I can answer, Linc hops back on his bike and straps his helmet on.

"What about our game?" I ask. I pass the basketball from my left hand to my right and back again. "Plus I need to tell you something."

"Later, okay? Can't play today. I've gotta go study." He pushes off before I can say anything else.

I watch Linc until he disappears around the bend. I guess I won't tell him about CSMHS today either.

Woomp, woomp, woomp. Stop, aim, and shoot. Clang. Off the rim. Is that H? If I'm playing by myself, can I even get H-I-P-P-O-P-O-T-A-M-U-S? Unclear.

Woomp, woomp, woomp. Stop, aim, and shoot again. No clang this time. No net either. Just a shot with too much arc and too little force, all adding up to an air ball.

Suddenly I don't care if it's H or I or any other letter. Without Linc talking on and on about cute girls and how hungry he is or seeing how loud he can burp, shooting baskets is no fun. It's just me, my pathetic shooting percentage, and the sort of ugly feeling that's settled in the back of my brain.

I'm happy for Linc. Of course I am. He's wanted to try out for the basketball team forever. And he's good enough. Really good enough, so he should make it—no problem. But I know I'm not as happy as a best friend should be. Linc thinks we'll be on the team together. But I don't think we will. Even if Coach Schwimmer gives me the job permanently, the team's statistical analyst won't exactly wear a uniform like the guys on the court. The statistical analyst won't sit on stage with the team at pep rallies either.

Linc will be "on the team," but I'll be more "with the team." It's different. And even if Linc doesn't think so now, I'm pretty sure it's going to feel different too.

Ten

The squawking of the PA system drowns out the slamming of locker doors—including mine. Mr. Dooley's voice drones out of the speaker above my head.

"Attention, students. Gabe Carpenter, please report to my office." The voice gets louder. "Gabe Carpenter. To my office, please." I flinch at the sight of every head in the hallway swiveling to stare in my direction.

I guess Mr. Dooley thinks the speaker is off because he clears his throat and lets out a muffled burp before it clicks off.

"What'd you do?" some kid I don't know asks as I walk down the hall.

I shrug. The answer is nothing. I didn't do anything. I have no idea why Mr. Dooley wants to talk to me. The last time I got called to his office was after I punched Cameron—and Maya. One thing I know for sure is that I haven't punched anyone lately. Or at all, since that day.

I shuffle into the outer office and stand there until Mrs. Francisco notices me.

"Go right in, Gabe. Mr. Dooley's waiting for you." She smiles at me, so whatever it is can't be that bad.

When I walk into Mr. Dooley's office, he's in the middle of taking a bite out of the biggest sandwich I've ever seen. Turkey, ham, cheese, lettuce, and tomatoes threaten to slide out from between the bread. He contains most of it, but a dollop of mayonnaise escapes and lands with a plop in the middle of his tie. Mr. Dooley doesn't notice. I pretend I don't either.

I linger just inside the door, waiting for him to finish chewing and swallowing. After a big slug of sweet tea, he motions toward the single empty chair. I sit.

"You're probably wondering why I wanted to see you." Mr. Dooley smiles. And when he does, I see there's a piece of lettuce stuck to one of his front teeth. It's a big piece and it's shaped kind of like Florida.

I smile back—without teeth—and shrug.

"Mrs. Capistrano and I were talking about your application to CSMHS."

"Okay."

"And I wanted to make sure you had everything you need." Another smile.

"I think so." Now the lettuce has moved from his tooth to his upper lip. It dangles there, flapping back and forth when he talks.

"You're our only applicant, you know." I didn't know for sure, but I thought I might be. "And I talked to Bitterman this morning. He's got eight applying this year. Eight."

Mr. Dooley runs his hand through his hair. Front to back and back to front. Bitterman is Mr. Bitterman, head of Overton Prep. They win everything. Or they did until last year's Academic Olympics.

"Wow. Eight is a lot."

"It is." The Florida-shaped lettuce migrates again. Back to the tooth. Mr. Dooley turns and takes a picture off the shelf behind him. It's a picture of him holding our first place trophy for the Academic Olympics.

I don't know what I'm supposed to say or really why I'm here. Maybe it's about the math. Because if eight kids from Overton are applying and CSMHS has a 28.75% acceptance rate, then two of them should get in. Well, 2.3 of them to be exact. But 28.75% of one St. Jude applicant—me—still rounds down to zero. Even if I *do* get in, that's only one. Any way you look at it, Overton wins.

"Um, I'll do my best." I glance down at my watch. Social Studies started ten minutes ago. And we're having a quiz. "I'm pretty late for class, sir, so . . ."

Mr. Dooley looks up from the picture. It's kind of like he forgot I was there.

"All right then. Good luck, Gabe. We're all counting on—I mean rooting for—you."

I scoot out of there as fast as I can. Poor Mr. Dooley. Anything to do with Overton Prep makes him crazy.

When the final bell rings, I head off in the opposite direction of every other student. It's also the opposite direction of the gym, where basketball tryouts start in exactly twenty-six minutes. I need to be there to keep track of everyone's stats. But I need to do something first.

By putting my head down and squaring my shoulders, I manage not to get knocked down or driven backward. Like a salmon swimming upstream, I finally make it to The Clubhouse.

"Gabe, come in." Sister acts like she was expecting me even though I didn't tell her I was coming.

"Hi, Sister. Is it okay if I talk to you for a minute?"

"Of course. Let's sit."

I slide into my regular seat and Sister Stevie sits next to me, at Linc's desk. She folds her hands and her ankles and waits. I stare at the bright pink high tops sticking out from below her long white habit. I start talking in the direction of those shoes.

"First, I was hoping . . . I mean, I wanted to ask if you could . . . Well, if you would do me a favor?"

"Probably, but it depends on what it is." There's a smile in her voice but I stay focused on the shoes.

"Well, I'm applying to CSMHS. The science and math high school. The application is pretty long. And there's a test—it's tomorrow—and an interview—that's later and only if I pass the test and my application is good enough." I force my eyes up until I'm looking at Sister Stevie. "The thing is, I need something from a teacher. You know, like a letter saying that you think they should let me in." Then I have a horrible thought. "I mean, unless you don't think they should."

"Do you want me to write you a letter of recommendation, Gabe?"

"Yes, please."

"I would be honored."

"You would?"

She nods her head vigorously enough to knock her veil forward. Sliding it back into place, she says, "I absolutely would."

"Everyone thinks I should go. Well, everyone who knows, anyway."

Sister Stevie reminds me of my grandma if Grandma was a lot younger, a little taller, and a nun. Sister has a slightly weaker version of the same superpower that makes me say things before I know I'm going to say them. Like now.

"But what do *you* think?"

Even though her superpowers probably mean she already knows what I think, I tell her anyway.

"I think it's awesome. I mean, you should see it. The science labs are so cool and you can learn any kind of math you can think of. They have all these teams and clubs for kids who like science and math. There's even a meteorology club." My words are coming out faster and faster. I turn and look out the window. "The kids were like me."

"It sounds wonderful. And like someplace where you could really grow and learn. So what's the 'but'?"

"Huh?"

"The 'but.' All that sounds great. It sounds like the right fit for you. And yet, you're not excited. There's no smile. So there must be a 'but.'"

I open my mouth to say there isn't one. That's not what comes out.

"It's far away. And I'd be the only one going. I wouldn't know anybody. And what about Linc? And Maya? And everyone else I've always gone to school with?" Then I almost whisper, "What if I don't get in? Or what if I do and I'm not good enough?"

Sister stands up and walks over to her desk. She roots around in the bottom drawer and brings back a picture. It's a bunch of girls in caps and gowns with their arms around each other and big, mostly dorky smiles on their faces. And one of them—the one with crayon yellow hair and the biggest smile of all—is wearing hot pink high tops.

"This is you?"

"Yep." Sister runs her finger back and forth across the girls' faces. "Me and my best friends at high school graduation."

"Cool."

"We had always planned to all go to college together. And they all did. But not me."

"Where did you go?" From the picture I can tell that Sister Stevie was the center of the group. She's right in the middle and the other girls are crowded around her. Sort of like she's the sun and they're the planets.

"The convent."

Duh.

"Oh."

"Yeah, oh. It wasn't the most popular decision I've ever made." Sister taps her finger on one girl in the picture. The one standing closest to her. "And some of them didn't understand. And even though I felt sure, I felt called by God, I was scared."

"You were?"

"Yep. Scared of the same things you are. Scared I wouldn't like them or they wouldn't like me. Scared that I couldn't do it. That it would be too hard."

"But it wasn't?"

"Sometimes it was. Sometimes it still is. But if it's right for you, it's worth it. Always."

I let that settle. Then I stand up to go.

"Thanks, Sister. You know, for saying you'll write the letter. And for the rest, too."

"You're very welcome." I head for the door and Sister starts erasing the white board.

"Oh, Gabe. I meant to ask how things went with Harry."

Harry.

I pause in the doorway and turn around.

"Um, not great."

"Really? What happened?"

"I'm pretty sure I did everything wrong. Nothing I did helped him at all."

"I doubt that very much," Sister says. "Gabe, you're just *part* of Harry's support team. Mrs. Winnegan told me you work really well with him."

"She did? But I don't know what to do." And here comes the truth. "What if I make it worse?"

"Gabe, you can't make it worse. I think you could make it a lot better," she says. "Trust Mrs. Winnegan. She'll help you."

I turn that over in my head a few times. "Mrs. Winnegan says that Harry's really smart."

"I'm sure he is."

"But he doesn't think he is," I say. "And if I had that much trouble spelling five words, I don't think I'd feel smart either."

"There are a lot of different kinds of smart, Gabe. Maybe you can help Harry understand that. You know, it can be hard to really see the truth about yourself when something's difficult for you."

"Yeah." Different kinds of smart. What does that mean?

Sister scrunches up her face and scratches her head through her veil. "Think basketball."

"What?" Now I'm really confused. Is she talking about tryouts?

"Think about you and basketball. And Gabe, remember to use your brain *and* your heart." She turns back around and starts erasing again. But this time she's humming.

My letter said the doors wouldn't be unlocked until "precisely" 8:30 a.m. According to my watch, which I synchronized this morning with the official time listed on the National Institute of Standards and Technology website, it's 8:24. Six minutes until we can go in. Twenty-one minutes until testing starts. And one hundred-eleven minutes until it's over.

Like any good scientist, I observe my surroundings. The first thing I notice is that most of the kids seem to be part of a group. Clumps of kids wait on the grass or on the front steps, talking or laughing or not talking, but all looking the same kind of nervous. There's a bunch of kids wearing Overton Prep T-shirts. I recognize most of them from the Academic Olympics last year. They're the biggest, loudest, and least nervous-looking group of all.

The hum of the van's window going down interrupts my thoughts about whether I should try to go to the bathroom before testing starts or if I'll be fine waiting until the first official break.

"Honey?" Mom packs a lot into that one word.

"I'm gonna go." I wave without actually turning around. I don't need to look at her to know she's wearing her "you can do it" face.

"I'll be right here when you're done."

"Okay." My legs seem happy to stay where they are.

"Gabe?"

I fill my lungs with as much air as possible, push off and head for the stairs. Shoulders back and head high, I make myself as tall as possible and pretend this is no big deal. That I've got this.

It's not until I get to room 214 that I realize I miscalculated. I should not have stopped at the bathroom on the way. Almost all of the seats are already taken. And all of the good ones are. I step to the side and check out my options. The best one seems to be a seat toward the back, sort of near a window. It's far away from the Overton kids and it's even behind a cute girl with dark hair that reminds me of Maya's.

I settle into the seat and smile back when the cute girl grins at me over her shoulder. Then it's time to set up. It doesn't take long since we're not allowed to use calculators or any scrap paper. For today, it's all about the pencils. I line up my five starters and make sure the second string is ready to go if I need them. Ten number 2 pencils, erasers fresh, lead sharpened to the perfect point—sharp enough but not too sharp; that leads to breakage. I feel my Saint Gabriel medal resting, warm and solid, against my chest. I'm ready.

Across the aisle, a kid with a nose a lot bigger than you'd want your nose to be chews on his thumbnails. Both of them. At the same time. I guess he's one of the nervous ones. The girl behind him is reciting formulas to calculate the area of regular polygons and the sums of their interior angles. She's nervous, too. The girl with the Maya-like hair is humming and twirling the end of her ponytail. Not so nervous, I guess.

The teacher plods up and down each aisle, handing out the tests—face down—telling us not to start until he gives the signal. I wonder if he's going to blow a whistle or sound a siren. Instead, once he hands out the last test, he stands in the front of the room and stares at the clock on the wall. We all do. At the exact moment the second hand touches the twelve, he simply says, "Begin."

And I mean to. Begin, that is. But when I pick up the pencil that's in the number one spot and start to write my name, I notice it. The smell. It's like broccoli soup mixed with Sabrina's noxious nail polish and a dose of egg salad sandwich gone bad.

Where's it coming from? I pretend to scratch my chin

with my shoulder so I can sniff my own armpit. Nope. Not me. Just smells like a pine tree—Mom bought me some new kind of "man" deodorant. I turn my head this way and that, sniffing. Feeling more and more like a bloodhound. My eyes water from the stench. I start breathing through my mouth but it's too late. It's already stuck inside my head—I can't unsmell this smell. *What is it and where is it coming from?*

"Ten minutes gone," says the teacher at the front of the room. He scans the room and goes back to reading his book.

The cute girl in front of me stretches her foot out into the aisle. Her bare foot. My eyes start watering double-time.

Ten minutes of test-taking time have elapsed. I've only answered one question and it's not even on the test.

Eleven

"Rebound! Rebound! Come on, get that rebound!"

Linc finally snags one by using his body to keep the other players out of reach. Coach calls it boxing out. Linc and I call it "letting your butt do the work." It's a move we've perfected playing driveway basketball.

The veins in Coach Schwimmer's neck stretch from his brick-red face to the neck of his sweat-soaked T-shirt. If anyone is listening from outside the gym, they'll think we're in the final seconds of a championship game. We're not. It's the first day of tryouts.

The only thing louder than Coach Schwimmer's voice is the squeak of twenty-five pairs of basketball sneakers jockeying for position on the court. Each pair is attached to legs that are jumping and running and straining to get a rebound. Any rebound.

I madly jot down who's making how many rebounds and what type—offensive or defensive—filling in my chart with dashes, dots, and squiggles, then filling in the final column with the appropriate value. I have a system. Quick mental calculations now, verification later. Coach is counting on me to accurately capture stats on each player. He'll use the information to help him decide who makes the team. And who doesn't. He'll also use it to decide if I make it onto his team permanently.

The whistle blows to end practice and the guys all rush toward the locker room. I make my last few notes and double check the stats of two players. One did great. Definitely in the top quartile. It's only day one of tryouts, but with a mere twelve spots on the team, the top quartile is a good place to be. The other one, who I thought would be alone at the top, isn't. I triple check my math, but statistics don't lie. Last year's number two player isn't even in the top fifteen. Weird.

"Hey, Linc!"

He turns toward the stands where I'm perched high enough to see all the action. Linc's hair stands up in tufts and sweat drips from his chin. Even from eight rows up, I can smell him. Well, him and the rest of the guys who are trying out. Sweat smells worse when you're not one of the sweaters. When you're sweaty too, it's like your own stink acts as a kind of buffer for your nose. I can't find any scientific evidence to support this, but I know it's true.

Linc waits until the last tired guy shuffles into the locker room. Then he beams at me and bounces up and down. "Wasn't that awesome? Incredible? Fantastic?"

I guess all of Linc's studying is improving his vocabulary. Or his understanding of synonyms, anyway.

"Yeah. It was great."

"How'd I do?" He gestures toward the notebook on my lap.

"Great."

"Really? Did I really do great?" He climbs up the bleachers, bringing his sweat smell with him.

"Linc, you know I can't tell you. I explained all that." I slap my notebook shut and stick it under my butt.

Before tryouts started, Coach Schwimmer had a talk with me about the importance of my role. He said he expected me to behave like a "professional" and a "valued member of the coaching staff." What that means is that if I want to keep my job, I have to keep everything secret. No one can know how they're doing compared to anyone else. This is the fourteenth time Linc and I have gone over this.

"Fine." Linc huffs out a giant breath and plops down on the bleacher beneath me. "I don't need your notebook, anyway. I know I was amazing."

Linc leans back and grins. And he's right. He *was* amazing. It looks like he had the highest shooting percentage, and his passing accuracy and performance during the agility drills were strong, too. The only part of his game that was less than stellar was rebounding. I don't mention that since I'm pretty sure part of the reason is because he's used to playing against me.

"So once I make this team and dominate for the season, it'll be on to high school and a starting spot on the Catholic Central freshman team." Linc smirks. "Or maybe even J.V."

"Wow. One good tryout and you're ready for the pros."

Linc laughs and elbows me in the shin. Instant bruise.

"Maybe. But first I need to get an A on my history test tomorrow." He stands up and starts back down the bleachers. "Are you coming?"

"To the locker room? No. That place smells like a buffalo's armpit."

"Wait for me then?"

"Yeah. There's something I need to tell you anyway."

"More meaningful glances from Maya?" Linc crosses his eyes and puckers his lips.

"Shut up. Meet me at the rock?" This long after school it should be deserted.

"Did you have to put your makeup on, too?" I ask. Linc takes longer to take a shower and get changed than my sister does. The cumulus clouds that were white when I sat down are now fully pink and the sun has started to set.

"Shut up." That's always Linc's comeback when I make fun of him for acting like a girl.

"So what do you want to talk about? *Is* it about a girl? Is it Maya? Or somebody else. I hope it's somebody else. Talking about Maya—well, you and Maya anyway—makes my brain hurt."

"It's not a girl."

Linc pretends to get up. I push him back onto the rock.

"Seriously, I need to tell you something."

"Okay, sorry. I'm listening." And he is. Finally.

"I'm applying to Carolina Science and Math High School."

"*What?*"

"CSMHS I'm applying. They invited me to apply. So I am. I went there on a tour and I took a test. A really hard test. I think I did okay, but I'm not sure."

Linc's not saying anything. Weird. So I keep going.

"They have a lot of really cool math classes and specialty science electives—even meteorology—and labs. It's a great school for kids like me. It's actually a school full of kids like me."

"So you're not going to go to Catholic Central?"

"I'm not sure. I might not even get into CSMHS."

"But you want to go there. Really?"

"There's a meteorology club. And it has twenty-six members."

"Seriously?"

"Yep. And the basketball team is really bad."

A thought that started back during the tour with Dr. Tremaine finally turns into something. And because he is my best friend, Linc thinks it too.

"So if they're that bad . . ." says Linc.

" . . . maybe I could make the team." I finish the thought and we both laugh.

Linc's laugh trails off first. We slide off the rock and start to walk in the direction of home.

"So what are the chances of you getting in?"

"They accept 28.75 percent of the applicants."

"That's not a lot."

"Nope."

"But you'll get in. I know you will."

"I hope so."

We walk two and a quarter blocks without talking. When we're almost to my house, Linc stops and grabs my upper arm.

"What?"

"You babbled about weather clubs and science labs and the bad basketball team. But there's one very important thing you didn't mention."

"What?"

"Girls." Linc grabs my other arm and gives me a shake. "Did you see any cute girls?"

The rest of the way home I tell Linc all about the one cute girl I saw. The one with the heinously stinky feet.

Twelve

I read over my application again. And again. It's done. I used my best penmanship. I answered every question as well as I could. I even figured out how to fill in three more of the blank lines for extracurricular activities. My analyst and statistician position with the basketball team was number two. Tutoring Harry was number three, even though I wasn't sure if something I was doing for service hours technically counted. And Maya reminded me that she and I worked on the canned food drive last year. So four lines out of five. Not perfect, but hopefully good enough.

I review my application checklist one more time. Applications are due on October twenty-fifth. Today is the twenty-first and it only takes one day for mail to get from my house to CSMHS. I verified that with the post office.

After I fold the application exactly into thirds, slide it into the envelope, and seal it, there's nothing left to do but mail it. And then wait.

Maya on one side of the table, me on the other, a plate piled high with cookies, and two glasses of ice cold milk—chocolate for me, white for Maya—between us. We've been here, just exactly here and just exactly like this, at least 200 times. Working on homework together at my house after school. So why does it feel different now? Why am I worried about how my hair looks? And why did I stand in front of my closet for ten minutes trying to decide what T-shirt to put on with my jeans?

"Are you going regular or semiregular?"

"Huh?"

"Your tessellation. Are you doing a regular or semiregular?" Maya points at me with her protractor. "I'm going semiregular."

Of course she is. Because putting together a semiregular tessellation is more than twice as hard as doing a regular one.

"Um, I guess regular." If I'm having this much trouble concentrating, it's probably best to go with the easier choice.

"Really?" Maya raises her eyebrows and does something with her neck to make her hair flip back behind her shoulders and then swing back and forth. It's kind of like Shelby's always-swinging-hair but with something extra. What does all of this mean?

I focus on the book in front of me. The varieties of tessellations on the page all start to run together. I randomly pick one and point to it.

"I'm going to do a hexagonal tessellation. It'll be tough enough." And with six sides and six angles to get right for each hexagon, it will be.

"If you say so. I'm going with a semiregular 4.6.12. Square, hexagon, dodecagon."

"Cool." And it will be.

I take my ruler and draw the first side of the first hexagon, then use my protractor to figure out the placement of the second line. It has to form an angle of precisely 120 degrees. If any of my measurements are wrong, the tessellation won't work. If I do it right, I'll have a series of polygons that cover a plane with no overlaps or gaps. And it will be able to go on forever. If I do it right.

Maya draws, calculates, erases, and mutters. The usual.

I draw, erase, think, erase some more, stare into space, and then draw the same line over again. Not the usual.

Maya starts to hum. At first it's kind of nice, but pretty fast it takes a right hand turn into annoying. I glance up and open my mouth to tell her to knock it off. But instead I find myself staring at her lips.

Maya used to chew on her lips whenever she was nervous or concentrating. So her lips always looked kind of dry and chapped. But not now. Ever since she started slicking on this pink gloss that smells like strawberries about a thousand times a day, her lips are always shiny. Which makes it hard not to stare at them. And then wonder things about them.

What would happen if I did more than just stare and wonder? What if I tried to be more than just friends with Maya? As soon as I let myself think the thought I try to unthink it. Fast. Because what if I did something wrong and screwed it up? I mean, Maya was mad—really mad— for months last year because I got a higher score on a stupid IQ test. What if I said the wrong thing, or did the wrong thing, or didn't do something I didn't even know I was supposed to do? What if I tried to hold her hand, but my hand slipped because it was all sweaty. Or what if I tried to kiss her and our noses smashed together or I missed or what if I was just really bad at it? What then?

How mad could she get and how long could she stay mad?

I use all my powers of concentration to focus on the paper in front of me. On my hexagon. After a few miscalculations, I get there. Six sides. One hexagon. Only about a million more to go. Since I'm taking the slightly easier road, I'll need to fill up the whole page to make this look impressive enough.

"I still don't get how this is art," says Maya.

She's almost done. Her work is precise and I can't see a gap or overlap anywhere.

"I'm not sure. I mean, it looks cool, but it's just a bunch of geometry," I say.

"Yeah." Maya looks up at the ceiling like the answer is written there. "But if Sister Stevie says it's art *and* math, maybe there's something else we're supposed to do." Her eyes snap back down and laser in on mine. "Do you think there is? Is there something else we're supposed to do?"

"I don't know. If it's art, maybe it's just what you want it to be. Like there's not a right answer." I wince as I say it because I know what's coming.

"No right answer?" Maya huffs out a big breath. "I thought this year was going to be different. We're actually getting a grade for G.A.S. class. And grades mean right answers and wrong answers. Or at least they should."

I can't think of anything to say so I just push the plate of cookies toward Maya—after I grab one for myself. She snags two and we munch for a while, letting the combination of chocolate and butterscotch chips work their magic. The line between Maya's eyebrows disappears and she relaxes the death grip she had on her protractor.

"Hey, how's your tutoring going?" I ask.

Maya shrugs and keeps chewing. "Good, I guess. Juliana got an A on her last math test." A slug of milk. "How about you?"

"Not so good."

"Why not?"

"Harry can't spell any better now than he could before."

"Seriously?"

"Yep." I shove a cookie in my mouth.

Maya tilts her head to the side. "Are you doing it wrong?"

"I don't know. Maybe."

I want to ask Maya for help. She knows stuff. A lot of stuff. Plus if her fourth grader got an A on a test, she must be doing it right. But before I can say anything, the side door slams and Sabrina and Becca walk into the kitchen.

"Oh, hey, Maya," says Sabrina.

"Hey."

"Are there any more cookies or did you eat them all?" This is for me.

"No, we didn't eat them all. They're next to the stove."

"Hi, Gabe." Becca sort of smiles at me and then looks away.

I want to yell or scream or something. Yes, I had a crush on Becca last year. Yes, I lost my mind—mostly because of Linc—and asked her on a date. And yes, she shot me down, which I'm reasonably sure wasn't just because neither one of us was old enough to actually go on a date. But I don't have a crush on her anymore. It went away about five minutes after I made a fool of myself. So how much longer will I have to feel embarrassed and humiliated all over again whenever I see her? Which, since she goes to St. Jude and is my sister's best friend and lives down the street, is all the time.

But not nearly as often as I see Maya. And that's enough of a reason to stop thinking about strawberry lip gloss.

Maya went home, but only after she got into a long—and boring—discussion with Becca and Sabrina about

hairstyles and whether Becca should keep tl
she bought or take it back. Since I couldn't t
thing I cared about less than that, I concentr
tessellation and actually finished it.

Now I'm hiding in my room to avoid any more "fasci-
nating" conversations Sabrina and Becca might be having. I take one last look at my homework before I slide it
into my G.A.S. class folder. It looks fine. I mean it fulfills
all the requirements of a tessellation. And my work is
neat. I made sure any eraser bits or pencil smudges were
cleaned up. The lines are clear and straight. The angles
sharp.

But it's not art. I don't even know much about art, but
I know this isn't it. Sister Stevie said art is supposed to
make you feel, and the only thing my tessellation makes
me feel is a little dizzy if I look at it too long. And even
though I didn't tell Maya—and I won't tell Maya—I don't
think her tessellation is art either.

I sprinkle a pinch of fish food on the surface of the
water. Celsius gets there first and swats at Fahrenheit
with one of his fins, trying to keep him from getting any.
No wonder Celsius keeps getting bigger—well, wider,
anyway—and Fahrenheit stays the same size.

I wait until the guys are mostly done eating before
bringing up what's bugging me.

"If Maya and I are supposed to be two of the smartest eighth graders, why can't we figure this out?"

Celsius isn't paying attention at all—he's too busy making sure he gets every last bit of food. But Fahrenheit flips around and swims toward me, like he's listening.

"So am I not the right kind of smart? Is art like girls? If I don't understand girls, then I can't understand art? But Maya is a girl and she didn't get it either. Is there some kind of art smart?"

Now Fahrenheit's not listening either. He waited around until one speck of food floated down from the surface and pounced on it. It's not like it's going to fill him up, but he twitches his tail. I guess that means he's happy for now.

I power up my computer and start looking up a bunch of stuff about learning and intelligence. Most of it is interesting. And the answer is yes, there are different kinds of smart. And there are also different ways of learning.

So now I know why Linc always talks to himself when he's trying to learn something new. Or remember something old. He's an auditory learner. He needs to hear stuff to really learn it. And I'm a visual learner, which explains why I'm always looking for answers on the ceiling. It's my way of looking around in my brain.

But it's the kinesthetic learning that I don't get. It's learning with your body. How can you learn math or reading or history with your body?

I remember Mrs. Winnegan saying something about Harry learning things differently. Maybe I should ask her what she meant.

"Gabe! Dinner!" My mom's voice and the smell of meatloaf wipe my brain clean of anything other than getting to the table. Fast.

Thirteen

It's been two weeks and three days since I talked to Sister Stevie about Harry. Two weeks and three days since she told me I was the right person to help him. That I needed to use my brain and my heart. Oh, and to think about basketball.

Well, two weeks and three days later I still don't know what to do. But I have to do something. I can't go there tomorrow and ask him to spell "panda" again. Because nothing I've tried so far has worked. So I know he's probably still not going to be able to spell it.

There's a part of me that feels like I'm cheating at service hours. I mean, if I'm not actually helping Harry, I'm not actually serving him or anyone else, right? I prayed about it during Mass this morning. I asked for the answer. Any answer. Well, as long as it's the right answer. We left church ninety-three minutes ago and so far—nothing. I can't wait anymore.

I pour two glasses of sweet tea and head out the side door. Because kneeling on the grass planting flowers around the base of the basketball hoop is someone who might be able to help.

"Hey, Mom. I brought you some tea."

"Thank you, honey. Just leave it on top of my stool." She doesn't look up from the hole she's digging.

I stay where I am, a glass in each hand.

My mom takes a pansy, places it in the exact center of a hole, and fills the dirt back in around it. She pats it down until it's perfectly smooth, first with a trowel, then with her hands. Finally, she takes off her gloves and glances up at me. Her eyebrows go up.

"Two glasses?"

I shrug.

"Actually, I was just about to take a break. Join me?" My mom clears a spot next to her on the grass.

We drink our tea for a while. Well, she takes a few sips and I drain mine. It's sort of cold today, and low, gray stratus clouds cover the sky. It's not raining—yet—but the grass is cool and damp enough to seep through my jeans and make my butt cold.

"You know the kid I'm tutoring?" I say.

"Harry, right?"

"Yeah, Harry." I start messing with the dirt my mom just finished arranging. She reaches over and rests her hand on mine until it stills.

"Mom, I don't know what to do. I don't think I'm the right person to help him. I mean, I'm *not* helping him. Every week it's the same thing. We have a list of five words. Sometimes he can spell some of them. For a minute, anyway. But most of the time he can't. And I can't make him spell them. So I think maybe I should quit. Do you think I should quit?" It all comes out in a rush.

"Wow," says my mom. "Well, I'm going to need some more information before I can answer."

"Like what?"

"Why do you think you're not helping Harry?" she asks.

"Because he still can't spell the words." I know I already covered that, but maybe she wasn't listening.

"And what have you been doing to help him learn how to spell the words?"

"Um, asking him how to spell them a bunch of times." All of a sudden I wish I had a better answer. But I don't. That's what I do. I have Harry look at the list and spell the words, then I take the list away and ask him to spell all of them. And he's never been able to. Not one time.

And sometimes I wonder if he's really trying as hard as he says he is. But I haven't said that to anyone but Maya. I'm not going to say it now.

"It sounds like you need to try something else." My mom takes her watering can and gives the new flowers a drink.

"Well, yeah. But I don't know what to try. So that's why I think maybe I should tell Sister Stevie I want to quit. There's got to be something else I can do for service hours, right?"

"What has Sister Stevie said?"

"She mostly said to listen to Mrs. Winnegan—which I am—and to trust that she knows what's best for Harry. Then she said to use my brain *and* my heart. And to think about basketball."

My mom tips her head to the side, then nods and takes another sip of her tea.

"That's good advice," she says.

"It is?"

"*Very* good advice." My mom picks up her trowel and starts digging the next hole.

Okay. That was not helpful. At all.

I go into the garage and grab a basketball. If I'm supposed to think about basketball, maybe this will help. I pass it from my left hand to my right and back again. Nothing. I dribble down to the end of the driveway and back again. Still nothing. I line up at the crack in the driveway we use for a foul line and go through my pre-shot routine. Woomp, woomp, woomp. Close my eyes and picture it going in. Since my mom's still under the basket, I skip the part where I shoot and it doesn't go in. But I don't think that matters. I don't get how thinking about basketball has anything to do with helping Harry spell.

"Help him see what he is good at," says my mom.

"Huh?"

"Harry may not be good at spelling, but everyone is good at something. Including Harry. Maybe you can help him figure out what it is."

"Okay." That feels like something that needs to sit in my brain for a while.

My mom gathers up all of her tools and heads into the garage to put everything away.

Woomp, woomp, woomp. Close my eyes. Picture the shot going in. And shoot. Clank. Splat.

"Woops. Sorry, Mom." One of the pansies she just finished planting is now flat on one side.

"I know you are."

She keeps looking at me. I'm not sure why. See, my mom is my mom but she's also a girl—well, I guess she's a woman but that's just someone who used to be a girl.

What that means is that sometimes I don't get her either. Like now. Does she want me to fix the flower? Can a flattened flower even *be* fixed?

"Did you know that Dad had a lot of trouble in school when he was young?" my mom asks.

"What do you mean?"

"I mean that Dad needed a lot of extra help with reading and spelling. It was hard for him. Sometimes it still is," she says.

"I never knew that."

My mom gives me kind of a sad smile. "He didn't want you to know."

"Why not?"

"He was embarrassed. He still is." She shakes her head. "Dad's a smart man. And he helps people. Lots of people. But I think there's a part of him that still feels ashamed."

My dad does help people. Every day. That's what a physical therapist does. And my mom's right. He is smart. He knows the name of every bone in the human body. He also knows all of the muscles and what they do. I'm still trying to memorize all of them. And my dad can fix anything. My mom jokes that she never gets to buy anything new like a vacuum cleaner or dishwasher, because my dad can always fix the old ones.

My mom grabs the basketball, dribbles twice, and takes a shot. Swish. She walks the ball over to me and, before she hands it to me, she grips my hand. Hard.

"Help Harry see what he *is* good at. It'll help make the other stuff matter a little bit less."

Stratus clouds don't lie. By the time I make three shots (which is after I've taken ten), rain has started to fall. Big, angry-feeling drops that bounce off the driveway—and my hair. I chase down my last rebound and dash inside.

"Can whoever that is hand me my adjustable, open-ended wrench?"

I skid to a halt in time. One more step and I would've tripped over both my dad's legs and his toolbox. The top half of my dad is under the kitchen sink.

"Sure." I try to sound sure. But when I crouch down and look into the depths of the toolbox, sure is the last thing I am. He said a wrench, right? So that means right away I can eliminate the things I know are hammers and screwdrivers. But that still leaves a lot of stuff.

"Uh, Dad? What does it look like?"

"Well, it's a wrench. And the end that looks like it does the work is open instead of closed." Okay. That helps. A little. "And there's a thing that you twirl with your thumb that makes the opening smaller or bigger." Bingo.

"Got it."

I hand my dad what I now know is the right tool.

"Thanks."

He goes about whatever it is he's doing. There's a lot of banging and shifting around. My dad really is too big to fit under the sink.

"Hey, Dad?"

"Yeah?"

"How do you know how to do that stuff?" It's a question I've wanted to ask for a long time. When my dad fixes stuff, he just does it. He doesn't need directions or instructions—somehow he just knows what to do.

The banging and shifting stop. But for a few minutes, nothing else happens.

"Come on under here."

"Really?"

"Yeah. Here, slide in." My dad pushes the other cupboard door open. I flip onto my back and slide my top half inside. It's dark in there. Or it would be if my dad wasn't wearing his head flashlight. It's a light attached to a stretchy band that goes around his head. It makes him look kind of like a miner. Or someone who exercises in the dark. I can't decide which.

"Mom said something was leaking under here. And when I checked, there was a puddle of water. A small one, but still a puddle." He turns toward me. I can't see his face because his headlight thing is shining right into my eyes. I can't see anything.

"What's leaking?"

"You've arrived at the perfect time. I'm just wrapping up my investigation." He sounds way more excited than a guy who's shoved himself into a small space should sound.

"I was right!" My dad slides out and sits up, stretching his neck this way and that. "It's the garbage disposal. We're going to need a new one."

"A new one? Can't you fix the old one?"

"Nope. It's cracked. You know, the average life of a garbage disposal is between ten and twelve years." My dad grins at me. "I put that one in when Mom and I bought this house—sixteen years ago."

He puts the wrench back and closes the toolbox, shoving it off to the side. "Hey, want to go to the hardware store with me?"

It's the kind of thing I usually say no to. Especially if I have homework—and I do. Or if I'm in the middle of a good book—and I am.

"Sure." I'm almost surprised when it comes out of my mouth.

"Really?" My dad sounds surprised, too.

On the way there, I ask my dad again, "So how do you know how to do all that stuff?"

"What stuff? Finding leaks?"

"Yeah. Finding them. And fixing them. And buildi ᵤ stuff—like that bookshelf you made me. That's awesome." I glance over at him. "Did I tell you it's awesome? And thank you?"

"You did now." He smiles and beats out a little rhythm on the steering wheel. "I guess I learned how to do all that by just doing it."

"I couldn't do that," I say.

"Sure you could. As smart as you are?"

"Not that stuff. I'd have to read about it. I'd need directions to follow and diagrams to study. That's how it works for me." It's true. Who else learns how to get better—well, a little better—at sports by reading about it?

"Huh. I see what you mean. I guess that's the way I've always learned. I need to touch things and feel how they work." My dad gnaws on his lip for a minute. "If I tell you something, do you promise not to tell Mom? Or Sabrina? Or anyone?"

"Okay."

"When I was in college, I had to take anatomy. And I had to learn the names of all the bones in the human body. Do you know how many bones that is?"

"Well, humans are born with more than 270, but an adult only has 206."

rs into the parking lot of the hardware
oot, and parks the car, before turning to

had to learn all of them. And memoriz-
ing things wasn't—isn't—easy for me." He blows out a big
puff of air like it's stressing him out to think about it. "So
I talked my professor into letting me into the lab at night
when everyone else was gone."

"What did you do?"

"There was a skeleton in the lab. It hung from a pole with
wheels. I would sit with my book in front of me and go
over each bone. I'd find it on the skeleton and trace it with
my fingers while I said its name over and over again."

"Wow. Did that take a long time?"

"A really long time. In fact, my buddies used to try to
figure out where I was all the time. I didn't want them to
know I was struggling, so I came up with a cover story."

"What was it?"

"Well, since I was spending so much time with the
skeleton, I gave it a name. Jenny." My dad chuckles. "So
when the guys would ask me where I was going, I'd just
tell them I was going to study with Jenny. They thought
she was my girlfriend." He smacks the steering wheel and
we both laugh.

"Let's go get that garbage disposal."

My dad had an imaginary girlfriend who was really a skeleton. Suddenly I'm glad I came along.

When we got back from the hardware store, I helped my dad install the new garbage disposal. Okay, I handed him a couple tools and got a towel when some nasty water spilled out of the pipe under the sink. But still, it was kind of like helping.

The whole time we were working on the disposal, something else was working in the back of my brain. I needed some time to figure it out. After a manly snack of boiled peanuts and pork rinds washed down with orange soda—because as my dad said, "You earned it," I told him I had some homework to do. Which was kind of the truth.

I flop on my bed and stare at the ceiling like the answer might be written up there.

Different ways of learning. Mrs. Winnegan said it. Sister Stevie said it. My research said it, too. I guess it just didn't totally click until today.

The way I learn is different from the way my dad learns. And different from the way Harry learns. But maybe the way my dad learns isn't so different from the way Harry does.

Maybe.

Fourteen

"Can we talk about something other than spelling today?" I ask.

Harry narrows his eyes. "What do you mean?"

"I mean all we ever do is talk about spelling. I thought today we could talk about something else. Okay?"

When I talked to Mrs. Winnegan about my idea, she said it was a good one. Then she helped me turn it into what I hope is an even better one. Still, I stopped by to see Saint Jude on my way out of school. Because even if it is a good idea, I could still mess it up.

"I guess." Harry sits back in his chair and crosses his arms in front of his chest.

"It's a little cold, but how about if we go outside?" I ask. "Mrs. Winnegan said it's okay."

Without waiting for Harry to answer, I walk out to the courtyard and plop down on a bench, my briefcase next to me. I unearth The Flog from the very bottom of the bag and document a couple episodes. Frequency, potency, volume—it all gets recorded. Things have been getting a little worse, so I started carrying The Flog around with me to make sure I capture as much data as possible.

I count by sixteens to pass the time. I get up to 544 before the door opens. Harry put on a sweatshirt but left it unzipped and hanging off one shoulder. He hops on one foot over to the other bench and jumps onto it.

Just as I start to close The Flog, I have to open it back up and record another entry. It's somewhat of a rarity—scoring high in both potency and volume.

Harry hops off the bench and stares at me.

"Was that you?"

Since I'm the only other person out here, there's no hope of denying it.

"Yeah. Excuse me."

"Excuse you? That was awesome. Can you teach me how to fart that loud? And wow, how do you make it smell that bad?" He plugs his nose.

I can feel my face get hot. "I don't have to try."

"Really?"

"Yeah, really." I tuck The Flog safely into my briefcase

before Harry has a chance to ask what it is. "Can we talk about something else?"

"Like what?" he asks.

"Stuff *you* like."

"Huh?" Harry jumps back down and stays still for the time it takes him to blink two times.

"We always talk about spelling, which I know is something you don't like. But we've never talked about what you *do* like." I smile—it feels too big, like one of those smiles my mom gives me when she's trying to convince me that this time I'm going to love cauliflower. I never do.

Harry bounces from one foot to the other and fiddles with the zipper on his sweatshirt.

"Donuts. I like donuts."

"Okay." I write down "donuts."

"And bugs. And superheroes. I really like superheroes. Some kids in my class—like Grace and Dylan—think superheroes are babyish, but they're wrong."

I reach into the inside pocket of my briefcase and pull out my lucky pen. The pen my grandpa gave me with the Superman S on it. I hold it out so Harry can see it.

"No, way. That's so cool," he says. "Can I touch it?"

"Sure."

But he doesn't. He stands in front of me with his hands

limp at his sides. "Sometimes I break things. I don't mean to, but sometimes it just happens."

"I know you'll be careful with this. It's my lucky pen." I hold it out again. This time Harry takes it and cradles it with both hands.

"What makes it lucky?" he asks.

"I'm not sure. It might be because my grandpa gave it to me. Or it might be because Superman is awesome." I grin at him and he shrugs back.

"Not as awesome as Spiderman."

"Why do you like Spiderman so much?"

Harry follows his usual path from the tree to the scraggly bush and back. Over and over. He talks while he walks.

"Well, he has super strength, of course. And agility. That means that he can jump and balance and walk in a zigzag really quickly when he needs to. Oh, and he's super fast, too." Harry finally stops pacing. But not talking. "And do you know about his 'spider sense'?"

"I think so, but I'm not sure," I say.

"Well, it's a different kind of smart. Not the kind like being good at reading and spelling and writing sentences. But the kind like he knows when something bad is going to happen or when something is wrong. And he fixes it." Harry's voice gets smaller. "He fixes things."

He fixes things. That's what Harry asked me the first day. If I could "fix" him.

Harry brings my pen back and hands it to me. He smirks. "Plus, with Spiderman, there's no kryptonite."

"Excellent point," I say.

"So are you like Superman?" Harry asks.

A laugh bursts out before I can stop it. "No." But I pause and turn the question around in my brain to see if there's even a smidge of Superman in me. "Well, other than the kryptonite."

"Really? Is it real kryptonite?"

"No. It used to be my locker. But now it's worse. It's girls." I make a "yuck" face and Harry makes it back. He starts giggling and doesn't stop until he falls over.

The door opens and Mrs. Winnegan sticks her head out. "Time's up for today, boys. It looks like you had a good time." She ruffles Harry's hair as he passes, then squeezes my arm. Her "thank you" is soft enough so that only I hear it.

Harry grabs his backpack from the closet and we start to walk out together. When we get to the door, Harry drops his backpack and ducks into the boys' bathroom. I turn around. "Mrs. Winnegan, I was wondering something."

"Yes, Gabe?"

"Can I make up some extra words for us to work on next time? Just a few?"

Mrs. Winnegan considers my question.

"More words, Gabe? I'm not sure that's a good idea. Harry is still struggling with the five words you're working on."

"I know." I chew on my lip. "I just thought maybe if we did something *other* than those same five words, maybe it would help." My voice gets smaller. "Because nothing is helping. Sometimes he can spell one of the words, or even two. But the next time I ask him—even if it's just two minutes later—they're gone."

"That's part of how ADHD affects Harry. You are helping, Gabe. I know it can be hard to see, but you really are helping." Mrs. Winnegan still has a thinking face on. "You know, I think working on some other words could be a good idea."

As soon as Harry comes out of the bathroom, he tears off down the hall to meet his mom. I walk slowly in the opposite direction thinking about donuts, bugs, and superheroes.

I finish writing up notes on all I learned about donuts. And bugs. Now I'm hungry and itchy. I can fix the hungry. It's the itchy that's going to have to go away on its own.

My not-so-deep, dark secret is that I hate bugs. I'm supposed to be a man—well, teenager—of science, and I hate bugs. I have an appreciation for nearly all scientific disciplines. Except entomology. It's the study of things that creep and crawl, sting and bite—things that *infest*, for heaven's sake. I just don't get it.

But Harry likes bugs. Maybe bugs can help him, since I haven't been able to. So I just spent an hour reading up on different bug species. Ugh. I scratch my head with my left hand and try to reach the middle of my back with my right. It doesn't help. The itches are still there. But so is the hungry.

I clomp down the hall to the kitchen and open the fridge. My stomach is overjoyed to see leftover fried chicken from tonight's dinner. I grab a leg and gnaw on it while pouring myself a giant glass of milk. The milk does a great job of washing down the three cookies waiting for me in the container of "imperfects." They're cookies that aren't good looking enough for customers but are good-tasting enough for family.

Sabrina is working at the kitchen table, books and papers spread all around her. Her hair is piled on top of her head in a knot with three pencils sticking out of it, and her left leg is jiggling at what I estimate to be 114 jiggles per minute. The evidence leads me to one conclusion. Sabrina's math homework is not going well.

"How's it going?" I brace for her answer. She does *not* want my help with homework. Ever.

Sabrina slumps back in her chair. The jiggling stops and she heaves a giant sigh. Finally, she glances up at me.

"I've almost got it. I mean I'm so close. But I just can't quite get the right answer. You know?" Then she scrunches up her nose. "You probably don't know, Mr. Super Genius." But the way she says it isn't as mean as usual.

"Are you kidding? The list of things I don't quite get wouldn't even fit on this table." I take a chance and slide into the chair across from hers. "What are you working on?"

"Word problems. Percent of change."

"Those are tough," I say. And they are.

"I know. It's like each one has three separate problems to figure out."

"Yep. What is the word problem actually asking? That's the hardest part," I say.

"Yeah. Then figure out what the equation needs to be and then . . ."

"Solve it." We say the last part together. Sabrina actually laughs. I do, too.

"Can I help?" I ask.

Sabrina looks at me and smiles with one side of her mouth. "Is it okay if I say 'no'?" she says. "I really think I'm close and I want to do it myself."

I glance down at her paper and immediately see where she's stuck. And how to get her unstuck. It would take less than a minute to explain. But she wants to figure it out.

"Okay. Good luck."

I start thinking about CSMHS and the presentation I need to prepare *in case* I get an interview. Of course I'll only get an interview if I passed the entrance test and if they liked my application. And those yeses (or noes) won't come for three to five more days. But I should be ready. In case. Only I don't have the slightest idea what to present about.

My head starts to itch again and so does my back. Which makes me remember things I learned about bugs. Which makes me think about Harry.

"Oh hey, Sabrina?"

"Yeah?"

"Can I have some of your old sidewalk chalk? I saw it in the garage."

"Sure. Whatever." She's already back at work, scratching a bunch of numbers down on her paper.

Fifteen

Linc chases me into G.A.S. class, still trying to put his stupid origami hat on my head. The thing looks like he stole it from a preschooler in a pirate costume. My hair does NOT need that kind of help.

"Knock. It. Off." I swat at his hand—again—and the hat sails through the air, coming to rest on the floor next to one of Sister Stevie's pink high-top sneakers.

Sister picks the hat up and examines it, turning it over in her hands before returning it to Linc.

"Hmm, nicely done. Very precise folding."

"Thanks, Sister." Linc places the hat on his own head like it's a crown, then winks in Shelby's general direction and sits down.

I just sit, then slide into a slump and wait to see what's next. Because Sister Stevie has that smile on her face. The one that means she's got "an opportunity" for us. Something she's sure will be fun and educational and altogether fabulous.

"Okay. Today is going to be fun. And exciting," says Sister Stevie. It looks like I was right.

"How many of you have been to an art museum? Or an art gallery?" she asks.

A bunch of hands go up. Mine isn't one of them. Linc's is. Maya's and Shelby's hands wave in the air, too.

"I've read lots of books about art museums," says Mary Frances. I wonder if Mary Frances ever actually does anything or if she just reads about it.

"Now, how many of you have ever participated in an art show?"

"Do you mean like as an artist?" asks Maya.

"Yes, Maya. That's exactly what I mean."

"Then, no. Not me."

A chorus of "Me, neither," comes from all over the room, including me.

"I have." It's Shelby.

"Wonderful," says Sister Stevie. "Would you please tell us about it?"

Shelby swings her hair and giggles. Was it a funny art show?

"Sure," she says. "Well, it was at a gallery in my old town. Every April they exhibited work done by students at my school." She ducks her head and giggles again, softly. "Last year, mine was in the window."

"That's wonderful," says Sister.

"What was it?" asks Linc. "Was it cooler than my hat?" He twirls it on his finger until it falls off.

"It was a bowl. I throw pottery."

"Throw it where?" asks Mary Frances.

"Like a bowl you eat cereal out of?" Cameron looks like his face hurts. I don't know much about pottery, but even I know that's kind of a stupid question.

"No, not that kind of bowl," says Shelby. "A bowl that you'd put on a shelf or in the middle of a table. It's a piece of art, not a dish." She turns toward Mary Frances. "And throwing pottery is just what it's called when you make something out of a lump of clay by spinning it on a pottery wheel."

I guess Mary Frances never read a book about pottery.

"Well, I'd love to see some of your work sometime," says Sister. "I'm sure we all would."

Shelby's cheeks are pink, but she's holding her head high—and still—and she's not giggling.

"This is wonderful. We have our own class expert," says Sister. "You all may want to get some advice from Shelby since . . ." Sister plays the air drums. I think she's trying to do a drumroll. ". . . you're all going to exhibit your work at this year's St. Jude Thanksgiving Art Show."

What?

"What?" asks Maya.

"We've had so much fun working on our tessellations and origami. I've been very impressed with some of your efforts. So I talked to Mrs. Quincy about displaying them with other students' art. I was just thinking that we'd put them out in the hall, but she had a better idea." Sister claps her hands. "She's invited us to exhibit in their show. Your projects will be alongside the art of her honors students."

What? My sweat glands instantly go into overdrive, making me wish I'd applied a double dose of deodorant this morning.

"Cool." Of course Linc thinks it's cool. "I'm totally doing origami."

"Okay, Linc." Sister walks over and plucks his hat off his head. "But you're going to have to do a little more than this to impress the judges."

"Origami's a total cop-out," says Cameron. "It's no harder than making paper airplanes."

"Really, Cameron?" says Maya. "You know, maybe this year it'll be me that punches you."

Sister spins around on one high-top sneaker to face Maya.

"Just kidding, Sister." Maya opens her eyes wide and tries to look sincere. "Really. I promise. I won't punch Cameron." Then she glares at Cameron. "But I will prove him wrong. I'm going to do origami, too."

"Anyone else?" asks Sister Stevie. Some of the kids pick fractals and others tessellations. There are a couple "I don't know yet" answers. One of those is mine. Because I don't have a brilliant idea. Or any kind of idea. All I really know is that something I make that's supposed to look like art but for sure won't is going to be on display in front of the entire school and parents and everything. It was bad enough last year when Sister made us write poems and read them out loud. At least the range of that humiliation was limited to the members of the G.A.S. class. This one potentially has no limits.

Linc's at his weekly check-in with Mrs. Capistrano. So far he's kept up his end of the contract. And with only two tryout practices left, it looks like he'll make the team, too. Not that I can tell him that. Even if he does ask to see the stats at least four times every day. And if the amount of time Coach spends poring over my stats is a clue, it's looking like my trial position might turn into a permanent one.

After I load up my lunch tray, I do the one thing you should never do in our cafeteria. Stand still. Standing still is like having a giant arrow pointing to your head that says "smack into me and make me drop my lunch tray and spew food all over the floor." Luckily, I realize my error and re-engage both my brain and my feet. With no Linc to sit with, my plan is to swing by Maya and Shelby's table and sit with them.

But when I come to the end of the middle table—the part they claimed as theirs the first day of school—I realize I'll need a new plan. Quick. Shelby and Maya's heads are so close together their foreheads nearly touch. A quick estimation tells me less than 3/4 of an inch separate them. And they're whispering. At the same time. Which is something only girls can do.

Maybe Harry's right and "spider sense" is a super power worth having. I must have at least a dollop because something deep inside my brain tells me to get away fast. I start to slink by. So far, so good. Neither of them notices me. Then I trip. Not spectacularly. I don't drop my tray, and even my straw stays put. But it's enough of a trip that my sneaker slaps on the floor when I catch myself. I sneak a peek over my shoulder—another tactical error—and see both girls staring at me. Shelby's face looks like my sister's when she plays with our neighbor's kitten. Maya's expression is unreadable. She looks confused, sort of. And her smile is kind of weird. Like she's smiling at someone who's definitely not me.

"Hey. Okay, well, I'll see you later." I start walking before I'm done talking. Before either one of them has a chance to tell me what they were talking about.

So it's just me for lunch. Well, me and today's special. And my presentation. None of it is quite right. No matter how many lunches I eat in the St. Jude cafeteria, I'll never get used to just how *not* special the specials are. Today it's ham steak and mashed potatoes. The potatoes are okay—a little lumpy and a lot gluey, but I can deal with that. What I can't do is make myself taste the ham steak. It's bright pink and there's some sort of shiny coating that looks sort of like jelly. And it jiggles exactly like jelly. My stomach growls and I tell it to be happy I talked Mrs. Vincent into giving me an extra roll.

I push the tray as far away from me as possible and look at the other thing that isn't what it should be. My in-case-I-need-it interview presentation. Well, technically it's not a presentation since it's just a blank sheet of notebook paper with the "CSMHS Interview" written at the top.

My brain churns through a bunch of words, trying to find some that sound impressive. Or at least make sense. I come up with four. When I look at the list, I start to feel kind of good about it. So I say them out loud, but low enough so no one hears but me.

"Inspiration, evaluation, dedication, innovation . . ." I pause, thinking there's something else.

"Perspiration. Constipation." A snort of laughter hits my ears at the same time a meaty hand slaps my shoulder.

"Whatcha doing?" asks Flick Phillips, the owner of the hand.

I slap my notebook shut. Any hope I had of making something out of a bunch of words is lost.

"If you're looking for Linc, he's not here yet," I say.

Flick flings himself into the seat next to me and leans in. Too close.

"I need your help," he whispers.

I lean back as far as I can without actually falling out of my seat. Flick is not acquainted with the whole idea of personal space.

"Why?" I ask.

"Coach just told me I might not make the team." Flick holds his head in his hands. "Can you believe that?"

The thing is, I can believe it. Flick was the number two player on the team last year, right behind Ty Easterbrook.

And since Ty graduated, you'd think Flick would be the number one guy. He's not.

"What did Coach Schwimmer say?" I ask.

"He said my shooting accuracy stinks. Well, he didn't say "stinks," but that's what he meant." Flick shakes his head. "I mean, I knew I wasn't making a ton of shots, but is it that bad?"

"You know I can't tell you," I say. "During the tryout period, the stats are strictly confidential."

"Yeah, he won't even tell *me*." Linc plops down across from me and crosses his eyes. "And I'm supposed to be his best friend."

"Shut up."

Linc grins and starts pulling food out of his brown bag. "What's wrong with you, Flick?"

"I stink."

"Well yeah, you always stink, but what's wrong today?" Linc cracks himself up. Flick's not laughing.

"Flick's worried about his shooting stats," I say. I give Linc the knock-it-off look I've perfected during the ten years we've been friends.

"So can you help me?" Flick asks. "You know, like you helped Ty with free throws last year?"

"Maybe."

"How? I'll do anything. Anything. Oh, and I'm sorry for

what I said about you when Coach made us do granny shots last season."

"What did you say?" Linc asks before I get the chance to say the same thing.

"Oh. Uh, nothing. I didn't say anything."

Even though Flick exhibits three textbook signs that a person is lying—avoiding eye contact, leaning away, and rubbing his ear—I decide to let him off the hook.

"How much did you grow this summer?" I ask.

"Four inches. Well, four and a quarter, to be exact. Why? Is that bad? I thought getting taller meant I'd get even better."

"Yeah, I thought that, too," says Linc. "Are you saying that getting taller is a bad thing?"

"No. Well, not exactly," I say. "In the short term, it can be a problem. But over time, yes, being taller is always going to be an advantage in basketball." I notice how Flick looks too big for the cafeteria tables. He has to scrunch his legs sideways to make his knees fit.

"Okay. So I have a short-term problem? Does that mean you can fix it fast?"

"It's not a fix exactly. It's science."

Linc rolls his eyes. "Of course."

"Do you want to hear this or not?" I say. "I have other stuff I could be doing." Like working on my presentation. Or figuring out what I'm going to do for the art show.

"Come on, Linc, I want to hear what Gabe thinks." Flick looks like he could cry any minute. That's a scene I don't want anything to do with.

"Okay. Now that you're taller, in order for your shots to go in, they require a different launch angle," I say. "I'm guessing your hands are bigger, too?"

"Yeah, I think they are." Flick examines his hands like they're not attached to the ends of his arms.

"Okay. So you might need to experiment a little to find your new optimal release point," I say.

"What does any of that mean? I've been playing basketball since I was five, and my hands and the rest of me have been growing the whole time. This has never happened to me before."

I grab my notebook and open it to a fresh page. A page that has nothing to do with my not-written-or-even-really-started presentation. And I start sketching. And talking. I take Flick and Linc through the research of Coach Bob Fisher and Dr. John Fontanella, two of the most exciting people—in my opinion—to study the physics of basketball. Some of it I have to repeat. Twice. But a lot of it they get.

"So I have to practice. Figure out the new release point and practice. Is that it?" asks Flick.

"And remember to keep your wrist in the neutral position. No radial and ulnar deviation," I say.

"Huh?" from Flick and Linc.

"Make sure your wrist doesn't wobble from side to side while you're shooting."

"Oh. Okay."

"I'm sorry it's not a quicker fix, but at least you know what's going on."

"And I'll fix it." Flick stands up and holds his hand out for a handshake. I expect him to try to crush my hand or to smack me in the arm. He doesn't. He just shakes my hand like he's giving me the sign of peace at church. "Thanks."

I have so much work to do. Regular homework. Finally deciding what kind of art project to try for the G.A.S. class art show—something that won't make me look stupid is my best idea so far. But first I check the mail. Because there wasn't a "yes"—or a "no"—in the mail yesterday. Or the day before. So there should be one today. According to the dates on my checklist, there should be one today.

The mailbox is empty. Sabrina. I bet she got there first. I race inside and toss my backpack onto the bench.

"Sabrina?"

Nothing.

"Mom?"

Still nothing.

I stop and listen. It's the kind of quiet our house only is when no one's home. Just to make sure, I swing through the kitchen. No Mom. No Sabrina. And no sign of any mail with my name on it.

When I go to grab a cookie, I see it. A note. It's written on Heavenly Bites chocolate-scented stationary in my mom's big, loopy handwriting.

Gabe—CSMHS called—your interview is November 10 at 4:00!!!!!! Love, Mom

They called. They want to interview me. Which means I passed the entrance test. And they liked my application well enough.

That's two more yeses.

Sixteen

Maya and I open the door to St. Jude Elementary and barely avoid being trampled to death by a herd of kinder-gartners. Those munchkins are fast. And strong. I grab Maya's arm and pull her against the wall next to me. We stay there until the kids have all gotten outside.

"Wow, they really want to go home," I say.

"Yeah. Me, too," says Maya.

"I thought you liked tutoring."

"Not really." She blows a puff of air up in the direction of where her bangs used to be. It's what she always does when she's thinking hard or worried about something.

"What happened?"

We stop in the middle of the hall, between the two

fourth grade classrooms. "Juliana doesn't really need any help. She's already good at everything. She just wants to be even better."

"So she's just like you?" It comes out of my mouth too fast for me to stop it. And Maya slugs me in the arm almost as fast.

"Ouch!"

Maya grins and walks inside.

Rubbing the spot on my arm where she connected, I turn and follow the sound of pencils pounding out a drum-beat. Outside the door to Mrs. Winnegan's room, I take a minute to get ready for Harry. I arrange my face into what I hope is a "you can do it" expression even though some-times I wonder if he really can. I mean he hasn't yet.

"Hi, Gabe! What are we doing today? Can we do something other than spelling again? 'Cuz that was fun last time even though I still think you're wrong. Spider-man is way cooler than Superman."

"Hi, Mrs. Winnegan," I say. She smiles and waves from where she's grading papers at her desk. I remember that she always used a purple pen. She'd draw smiley faces and suns next to our work, even when it wasn't totally right.

"Hey, Harry. We're going to have fun today. Some of it is spelling and some of it's not."

Harry hits me with a fierce look. At least I think it's supposed to be fierce. "You promise it's going to be fun?"

"Yep. Promise." I head for the courtyard. "Are you coming?"

Harry follows behind me, so close that he keeps stepping on the back of my shoes. When we get outside, I start to unpack while Harry practices walking on his hands. He's really good at it.

"Hey, can you do this? I bet you can't. And you know what, I bet Superman can't either. But Spidey totally could. I mean, he spins webs and swings between buildings and stuff."

Harry doesn't seem to mind that I only answer some of his questions. There are just too many and they come so fast.

I get out Sabrina's sidewalk chalk and get to work.

"You brought chalk? Cool. Can I make a picture? I can draw a really cool dragon. Want to see?"

"How about we draw dragons after?" I say. "Actually, you'll have to teach me because I don't know how to make a dragon."

"You don't? I thought you could do anything."

"Nope. Can't draw a dragon. I can't draw much of anything."

Harry flips back to his feet. "Wait a minute. You wrote words."

"Yep."

"I thought you said we were going to have fun?" Harry wraps his arms around himself.

"We are."

Yeah, he doesn't believe me. At all.

"I promise this will be fun," I say. "Look, I'll even go first." I saunter over to the first letter on the sidewalk and stand at the top, thinking about everything I read—and everything my dad said—about kinesthetic learning. "I'm going to follow the path this letter takes with my feet." I start at the top and go down. Then back to the top and make a sideways half-circle and then another. B.

"Can I try?" asks Harry.

"Of course."

He runs over and starts to race down the line and totally skips the first half-circle. And he doesn't tell me the name of the letter.

"Okay. Can you do it slower this time?" I have a sudden brainstorm—or maybe it's an answered prayer. "And if you match just what I did, when you're done, you can tell me something about bugs." I hold myself still as a statue to hide the fact that just the word "bugs" gives me the shivers.

"Really? Cool. 'Cuz I know what I'm going to tell you. It's about my favorite bug—well, favorite animal really—in the whole world."

"Okay. But after. I'll do it again first."

I walk the path of the B again, making sure to take slow, precise steps. This time, Harry does much better. He only has to go back to the beginning twice, and he even remembers to tell me the name of the letter.

We repeat the same steps for the U and the G. When Harry comes to the end, he says, "B. U. G. That spells bug."

"Fantastic!" I hold my hand up for a high five.

"I did it!" Harry launches into a celebration dance. "But wait, why did you ask me such an easy word? Even *I* can spell 'bug.'"

"Because I want to make sure I do this right, okay?"

Harry shrugs.

"So, your favorite bug, right? Go ahead, tell me." I make sure to face Harry, giving him all of my attention.

"Have you ever seen a rhinoceros beetle?" he asks.

"I don't think so."

"Then you haven't. Because if you had seen one, you'd know it. I've only seen one once—it was last summer in my back yard. You should have heard my mom scream. I think she even peed her pants a little bit, even though she said she didn't. She said she sat in some water while she was pulling weeds. But I know that wasn't true. She peed her pants."

And even though every part of me doesn't want to ask, I go ahead and do it anyway. "What makes it so scary?"

"Well, it's pretty big, as bugs go. They can be up to six inches long. But that's not the best part. The best part is that they have horns. Horns!"

Harry's hands and fingers fly as he gestures to make sure I get what he's saying. Oh, do I. He's talking about a giant bug with horns. No wonder his mom wet her pants. I'm pretty sure I would too.

"What else?" I ask.

"I guess my favorite thing about it, other than how totally fierce it looks, is how strong it is. Did you know it's the strongest land animal for its size? It is. It can carry eight hundred and fifty times its own weight. And they can't bite or sting, so you totally don't have to be afraid of them. They just scare predators away because they *look* ferocious. Oh, and they hiss. Like this."

Harry starts walking toward me and hissing. I remind myself that I'm trying to help him. That this might work. I tell myself it's worth it. That I probably won't have nightmares about giant, hissing bugs with horns for too many nights in a row.

"I think the next word we'll work on is 'horn,'" I say. "How does that sound?"

"Cool."

"You know, Harry, you're really smart about bugs."

"I am? Really? I have lots more stuff to tell you, too."

Harry leaps onto and off of the bench closest to me while I write "horn" in giant blue letters. When I finish the last letter, I make myself a promise.

Next week we're talking about donuts.

Seventeen

"Hey, Gabe!"

I turn around and see Flick waving his hand in the air. He catches up to me in three giant strides. The smile that splits his face in two makes me think he has good news.

"What's up?" I ask.

"Well, I thought about everything you said about my shooting. Well, the parts I could remember, anyway. And I tried it. I did what you said."

"Did it work?" It should've worked. Based on all the research and all the science, it really should have worked.

"I practiced for hours every day. Until way after dark. I only stopped when Mrs. Newsome next door told me she was going to call the police," says Flick.

"For shooting baskets?"

"Yeah." He grins. "She said the sound of my ball bouncing on the driveway was making her crazy."

"So?" I ask.

"So what?" Flick says. "Oh, so yeah. It totally worked. It took forever to figure out my new shot. But once I did, I practiced it like a million times. And I've got it. Just wait 'til tomorrow."

I hope Flick's right. Tomorrow is the last day of tryouts. And at the end of practice, Coach Schwimmer is going to announce who makes the team.

I finally get to my locker. My dad is picking me up in eight minutes. Today's the day of my interview. The last hurdle between me and a "yes" from CSMHS.

I twirl the combination to my locker and lift the handle. Nothing. It doesn't open.

IT DOESN'T OPEN.

Okay, don't panic. I'm sure I just missed one of the numbers. I square my shoulders and face my locker again, head on. Breathe in, breathe out, and go. 27 right, 12 left, 2 right. Listen for the click and lift. Still, nothing. For the first time since last year, my locker won't open.

My stomach clenches. Does this mean something? Is it a sign? I send a prayer up to Saint Jude—a quick one. It's all I have time for. Then I stare at the combination on my locker. Two things my grandma says run through my mind on a loop. "Third time's a charm," and "Three strikes and you're out." Which is it going to be?

My palms are slick with sweat. So are my pits, but at least I don't need those to open my locker.

Again I turn the lock—27 right, 12 left, 2 right. Come on, open. Please. Just open.

It opens.

My whole body goes limp with relief. Including my intestines. I don't have the energy to even try to muffle the unmistakable sound and smell of gas leaving my body. Brett Canfield, whose locker has been next to mine since the beginning of sixth grade and who has never said one word to me, turns and snickers. "Nice one."

Yeah, great. Nice one.

My dad will be here in three minutes. I've got to go. I grab the books I need for homework tonight. Homework I'll do after Dad and I get back from my interview.

Dad. He rescheduled his late appointments so he could take me today. He's probably already out front. I slam my locker door shut and take off down the hall, falling in with a sea of other kids leaving school. When I finally get outside, I see two things. One is my dad's car at the curb. The other is Linc and Maya talking by the rock. Linc is talking and laughing and Maya is looking annoyed, which is how she usually looks around Linc.

I start walking toward them because they're on the way to my dad's car. Linc doesn't see me yet. But Maya does. She stares at me—there's no other word for it—almost like she's daring me to look away. Then she goes up on her toes and kisses Linc. ON THE LIPS. And, wait—hold on—it looks like he's kissing her back. He is. HE'S KISSING HER BACK.

Maya kissed Linc and he kissed her back in front of the entire school. In front of me.

"So, are you excited? Nervous? Don't be nervous. You'll do great." My dad starts talking as soon as I collapse onto the front seat of the car. He reaches into the backseat and drops a brown paper bag in my lap. "Oh, Mom packed you a snack. Nothing messy—wouldn't want to slop anything on your shirt—just some apple slices and trail mix. Some good brain food. Oh, and a water to keep you hydrated."

I grunt and take an apple slice out of the bag. But there's no way I can eat it. I just hold it in my hand and stare out my window at the never-ending line of pine trees that follows the curve of the road.

It's not until we get to CSMHS and I go to get out of the car that I notice what I've been stepping on the whole way here. The binder with all of my notes and practice questions and answers. And my presentation. That's what I was supposed to be doing during the drive. Practicing for my interview. And eating a healthy snack, of course. Instead, I spent the whole time trying to figure out what I saw. Maya kissed Linc. And Linc kissed her back. No matter how many times I say it in my head—and see it in my head—it still sounds like a joke. But it didn't look like a joke.

But now we're here. It's time for my interview. So I grab the binder and shove it into my briefcase.

"Ready?" asks my dad.

"I guess."

Which is a lie. I'm not ready. I was ready—earlier today even I felt like I had this. I mean I went over every practice question I could think of six times. Enough to be sure I had an answer, but not so much that it would sound like I memorized them. And my presentation is solid. I'm sure about that.

"Okay, then. Good luck. I'll be waiting right here when you're done."

My dad straightens my collar and tries to flatten down my hair. I'm not too hopeful that he has any success since he's never been able to make his own hair—which is exactly like mine—lay flat.

"I'm fine, Dad." I climb out of the car, dragging my briefcase with me.

The front doors of CSMHS appear bigger today than they did the morning of the testing. Or the day my dad and I took our tour. When I try to open one, it feels bigger, too. And heavier.

I find the room where I'm supposed to be—the Galileo Room. The door is ajar. I hear voices coming from inside. I check my watch. Three minutes until my scheduled interview time. I stand against the wall, close my eyes, and breathe. Over and over I breathe. And pray. I feel for my medal through my shirt and try to imagine what my grandpa would say to me. I can almost hear his voice. Almost. But then someone inside the room laughs—a big, loud laugh that sounds like Linc.

Linc.

Maya.

Kissing.

"Gabriel Carpenter?" A man steps out of the Galileo Room and holds out his hand. It takes me a minute to reach my own hand out to shake his.

"I'm Dr. McNeely. I teach trigonometry and calculus. Dr. Tremaine is inside. Are you ready?" He smiles.

A praying mantis. Dr. McNeely looks just like a praying mantis—tall enough to have to duck when I follow him into the room and so skinny his pants would totally fall down if he wasn't wearing a belt. And suspenders.

Dr. Tremaine barely looks up when I walk in.

"Take your seat, please," he says.

"Okay." I slide into the seat that's by itself on one side of the big table. Dr. McNeely sidles around to the other side and folds himself into the chair next to Dr. Tremaine.

Dr. Tremaine doesn't look like the same person who gave me my tour—and a T-shirt. The person with the big smile who seemed sure I'd be here next year as a student. This version of Dr. Tremaine is stone-faced and doesn't give a hint that he's ever seen me.

Gulp.

"Dr. McNeely will ask you some questions first. Please take your time with the answers. Then you'll have time for your presentation." Again, no smiling.

All of a sudden, every sweat gland in my body goes into overdrive. My palms are instantly damp. Ditto my pits. I scratch behind my ear and find even my scalp is sweating. My stomach clenches.

Dr. McNeely's questions go on for a while. A lot of them are enough like the questions I practiced to make me feel like I'm doing okay. Maybe not great. Saying "um" a bunch probably isn't such a good thing, but I'm getting the answers out. Dr. McNeely smiles at me before and after every question, and Dr. Tremaine's face even starts to relax. Nothing you could call a smile yet, but the I-really-need-to-go-to-the-bathroom look he had on his face when I walked in is gone.

After the last question, they both scribble a bunch of notes. It takes a while and there's no other sound in the room besides the scratching of their pens on paper. What are they writing? Were my answers okay? Did I sound stupid? Maybe they do take points off for saying um. Or for sweating too much. Or for having bad hair. Major clench.

Dr. McNeely and Dr. Tremaine put down their pens in unison. Both pairs of eyes focus on me like lasers.

"Whenever you're ready, you may begin," says Dr. Tremaine.

I'm not sure if I should sit or stand. Standing seems a little goofy since there are only two other people in the room, but sitting feels wrong somehow. So I slide my chair back and try to make myself look as tall as possible. There's all kinds of research about how tall people seem more confident and knowledgeable. I'm not tall—not even a little bit tall—but if I stretch myself up as high as possible, and especially with them sitting down, maybe I'll seem tall. Or tall*ish*, at least.

The guidelines for the presentation were to show—in fifteen minutes or less—how you've used math or science creatively to meet a need or help solve a problem. I reach down into my briefcase and unload my presentation and supporting data. It's the same presentation—with a bunch of extra stuff—that I gave to Coach Schwimmer.

Two more deep breaths—in strong through the nose and out slowly through the mouth—and I feel ready. Mostly. I glance around the room, wishing for a window to look out of. But there's nothing but plain gray walls. On the wall opposite where I'm standing is a framed poster of the Galilean moons, the four satellites that orbit Jupiter, and a sliver of the planet itself. I mumble the names of the moons under my breath—Io, Europa, Ganymede, and Callisto—and start.

"Rebounds, shooting accuracy, speed up and down the court, free throw accuracy. All of these, and more, determine how successful a player will be on a basketball team. Or even if that person should be on that basketball team." Dr. McNeely sits up straighter. I try to ignore the fact that he's taller sitting down than I am standing up.

"I love basketball. I always have. I like watching it and I like playing it." Ignoring the fact that my stomach is doing front and back flips, I keep going. "The problem is, I'm terrible." I grin. "Like really, really terrible."

Dr. McNeely chuckles. Dr. Tremaine doesn't. Which makes me wonder if maybe he stinks at sports, too. And maybe he doesn't think it's funny.

"I've always wanted to be on a team. A basketball team." It's true. "I never tried out though—never even told anyone I'd want to try out—because I knew I wouldn't make the team." Also true. "So I mostly just play driveway basketball with my best friend Linc and think a lot about what makes someone good—or bad—at basketball. I came up with a bunch of metrics and started keeping statistics."

I pass three notebooks full of raw data across the table. It's my supporting documentation. Then I present Dr. McNeely and Dr. Tremaine with their own copies of the results.

"At first I just collected data for fun. But then I started to see how useful it was. And how useful it might be to our coach. Coach Schwimmer's the head basketball coach at St. Jude." My stomach starts to unknot and my palms are almost dry. It's going pretty well. I think.

"So I asked Coach Schwimmer if he could use me—and my analysis—on the team. At first I think he thought I was crazy." Dr. McNeely chuckles. "But then he looked at the stats. When he saw what I'd done, he offered me a job." It wasn't quite that easy. "Well, not at first. And there's no pay so I guess it's technically not a job. But I am the team analyst and statistician." I can't stop the smile that spreads across my face. "I'm on the coaching staff."

Both men start flipping through my notebooks. Dr. Tremaine flips quickly at first, then slows down and seems to really study it. Dr. McNeely opens to a random page and starts nodding right away.

"Tomorrow is the last day of tryouts. I'll be presenting this information to Coach Schwimmer. It'll help him decide which of the guys ends up making the basketball team." I relax my body, losing at least two inches in the process.

"Nicely done," says Dr. McNeely. "I hope Coach Schwimmer is as impressed as I am."

"Thank you."

Dr. Tremaine still hasn't looked up from the page he's on. I crane my neck to see what it is, but his arm blocks my view.

"What exactly is 'chair air'?" he asks.

"Excuse me?"

"Chair air. What is it?"

This can't be happening.

"Let me see that." Dr. McNeely grabs the notebook and starts reading. He flips a few pages forward and back, his lips moving along as he reads. "This certainly is creative."

"Can someone explain to me what this data is and what it has to do with basketball?"

"It was a mistake," I say.

"It doesn't have anything to do with basketball," says Dr. McNeely. "But it's a terrific study of the causes and effects of flatulence. The data is very thorough and well analyzed, and some interesting conclusions have been drawn."

The sweat is back—worse than before. And the clenching has moved from my stomach lower. It's all I can do to stay standing.

"So, then, it's a notebook about . . . intestinal gas?" Dr. Tremaine looks confused. Or annoyed. Probably both.

"Yes, sir."

"I think we're done here." Definitely annoyed.

"Thank you." I gather up my notes and shove them into my briefcase as fast as I can; my only goal is making it out the door. Fast.

"Oh, and John, chair air is a kind of gas event. The kind when your derriere nearly lifts right off your chair." Dr. McNeely barely keeps a straight face while he's explaining it to Dr. Tremaine. Then he gives up and guffaws.

My hand is too slippery to turn the doorknob. So I'm trapped. Here in this room where I just gave The Flog to one of the people who decides if I get into this school.

I turn back around and face them.

"Um . . ."

And it's then that I finally get what Linc means by "meaningful glances." Because sometimes there can be a whole lot of meaning packed into one look. The one Dr. Tremaine just gave me, for instance, means "there is no way this kid is getting into this school."

Why hasn't anyone invented a time machine that works yet? People invent stuff every day. So why not a time machine? Because that's the only thing that could fix what just happened.

I'd use it to go back to this morning and not go to school. I'd stay home and practice for my interview, steering totally clear of anything to do with St. Jude Academy Middle School and the rock. Then I never would have seen Maya kiss Linc and Linc kiss her back. And if I'd never seen that, I wouldn't have been distracted on the way to my interview. If I hadn't been distracted, I never would have just shoved my presentation into my bag where it got tangled up with all my other school work. And The Flog. I never would have given Dr. Tremaine The Flog.

But I did.

My face must look exactly like how I feel Inside. Because when I open the car door and get in, the smile slides off my dad's face and whatever question he was about to ask me never gets past his lips. Instead, he turns on the car and starts driving.

When we get home, my dad steers around a car parked in our driveway.

"Grandma's here." It's the first thing he has said. He starts to say something a few times; there is a lot of throat clearing. But he never actually says anything. Neither do I.

"Can you tell her—and Mom—that I don't feel good? And I'm really tired?"

My dad doesn't answer.

"Please, Dad?"

He puffs out a big breath and opens his door. "Okay."

I open the door into the house and speed walk through the kitchen, waving a hand in the direction of my mom and grandma but not stopping or saying a word. I'm almost to my room when I sneak a look back over my shoulder. Big mistake. My grandma is standing at the other end of the hall looking at me. She looks worried. And something else. She looks sorry for me.

She knows.

I didn't say a word and she knows.

And if my grandma knows, then for sure somehow my grandpa knows.

I let him down.

Lying down on my bed staring up at the ceiling, I realize something. This is officially the worst feeling I have ever felt. Worse than the time Sabrina slammed my hand in the van door. Worse even than the time I slid down the climbing rope in gym class and got second degree rope burns (that was my do-over after I broke Coach Schwimmer's toe). It even feels worse than when I accidentally punched Maya while not-at-all accidentally punching Cameron.

Across the room, on the wall next to my "application checklist," three scraps of paper are pinned to the wall. Each scrap has one word scribbled on it—"yes."

I only needed one more yes.

Eighteen

Hiding in my room until my grandma left and everyone else went to bed seemed like a great plan. And it
kind of was. At least until I realized that I neglected to
factor my bladder into the equation. I drank an entire
twenty-four-ounce bottle of water on the way home just
to give me something to do other than cry or blurt out
to my dad what happened.

And now it feels like there's way more than twenty-
four ounces of something wanting out of my body. Now.
I try thinking about dry things. The desert. Sandpaper.
My mouth when a cute girl—or any girl, really—walks by.
It doesn't help. I'm going to have to go out.

I ease the door open—slowly—so it won't squeak. To get

to the bathroom, I have to pass Sabrina's room and cross the hall. I pad down the hall as silently as a ninja, holding my breath all the way. Once inside the bathroom, I close the door—again without making a sound—and go about getting rid of that bottle of water. I brush my teeth while I'm there. Then it's time for the return trip.

I press my ear against the door. The voices I hear are faint enough to mean everyone's still in another part of the house. I make it back to my room and am about to slip inside when I see it. There's another note on the outside of my door. I can't be sure, but I don't think it was there when I left.

Linc called. Meet him at the rock before school. Love, Mom xoxoxox

I don't meet Linc at the rock before school. I don't meet Linc anywhere before school. Or during school. In class, I pretend I don't see him. Or hear him. And at lunch, I grab the granola bar and apple I stashed in my locker and have lunch with Saint Jude.

It's not like I can avoid Linc forever. But I don't want to talk to him yet. I don't have to talk to him yet. But I do have to talk to Coach Schwimmer. We have a meeting before the final tryout.

Even though I can see him through the glass, I knock on Coach's office door and wait for him to wave me in.

"Hey, Gabe."

"Hi, Coach." I sit down and pull out the same presentation I gave to Dr. Tremaine and Dr. McNally yesterday. Minus The Flog.

"Okay, let's go over all this one more time," Coach says. He flips and scribbles and mumbles. "I've got my list of twelve, but I want to make sure it jives with your list." He looks up from my largest—and coolest—graph. "You do have a list, right?"

"Of course. That's the last page."

Coach flips to it and compares my team roster with his own.

"It's a perfect match." Coach grins.

"That's good, right?"

"Gabe, do you own a tie?"

Huh? Did I miss something?

"Uh, yeah. I mean yes, sir. I've actually got two." One of them is a Christmas tie, but I guess it still counts.

"Good. Because on game nights, all members of my staff are required to wear dress shirts and ties."

"Game nights, sir?"

Coach Schwimmer stands up and reaches out to shake my hand. "Congratulations, Gabe. You earned it."

I can't wait to tell Linc. But I'm not talking to Linc. I bet my dad will be excited, though. Maybe not as excited as he'd be if I was actually one of the players, but still.

"Now comes the tough part," he says.

"Sir?"

"We filled twelve spots. But there are a lot more than twelve boys in the gym hoping to hear their names." Coach pops his fist on the doorjamb as he walks out. "The tough part."

Coach Schwimmer asked me to skip the part where he announced the team roster. He said some kids get really upset and sometimes even cry. And he didn't want to make it any worse by having any extra people there. That means I didn't get to hear Coach call Linc's name. I didn't get to see him give Linc his jersey. But I didn't have to be there. Linc's my best friend. And he wanted this more than anything. I didn't have to be there to know.

Just like I don't have to turn around to know that the footsteps coming up the driveway are Linc's.

Woomp. Woomp. I close my eyes and picture myself making the shot. Release and—swish.

"Whoa. Great shot."

"Thanks."

I snag my own rebound and start lining up another shot.

"We're not playing H-I-P-P-O-P-O-T-A-M-U-S today?" asks Linc.

"Guess not." I take another shot. Clang. Off the rim. I grab the ball and get ready to try again. "So, congratulations on making the team."

"Thanks." Linc walks around and stands in front of me. "You, too. Coach said you're officially part of the coaching staff. That's awesome."

"Yep. Awesome."

I flip the ball to Linc. Instead of taking a shot, he passes it from his left hand to his right and back over and over again, keeping his eyes on the ball.

"So, you're mad at me." Totally not a question.

"I guess."

"You heard about Maya kissing me?"

"I *saw* Maya kissing you." Linc's head snaps up. "Yeah. I saw her kiss you and I saw you kiss her back."

"Oh."

"Why did you kiss Maya? And what did you do to make her kiss you?"

"Okay, so I don't have *any idea* why she kissed me. We were talking about our origami projects—she said my idea was immature and stupid. Which it wasn't. And then all of a sudden, she leaned forward and kissed me."

It sounds random and confusing and totally illogical. In other words, a lot like Maya since the beginning of the year. So yeah, it could've happened that way.

"But that doesn't explain why you kissed her back." I reach out and smack the ball out of Linc's hands.

Linc looks up at me and tries not to grin. But he can't help it. "A girl kissed me, Gabe. It didn't matter if it was Maya. It was a girl. Kissing me. There's no way I could've stopped my lips from kissing her back."

Now it's me that tries not to smile. Because he's right. Linc would never not kiss a girl back. Even if that girl was Maya.

"Can we stop talking about girls and play some H-I-P-P-O-P-O-T-A-M-U-S?" I line up at the foul line, dribble twice and send the ball toward the net, granny-style. Swish.

"Your shot."

Linc takes his free throw shot overhand. The ball takes a trip around the rim before falling in.

"Hey, wasn't your interview yesterday?"

"Yep."

I take what should be an easy layup. Instead, the ball lips out and flattens yet another of my mom's pansies. I grab it and lob it to Linc, then try to make the flower look a little less flat.

"How'd it go?" Linc makes the same shot with ease. That's H on me.

"Looks like I'll be at Catholic Central next year." I concentrate on propping the flower up by packing some extra dirt and mulch around its base. Now instead of looking flat, it's just sort of leaning to the left.

Nineteen

I trudge across the parking lots that separate St. Jude Middle School from St. Jude Elementary School. The gray, heavy-looking cumulonimbus clouds and low barometric pressure combined with my mood make it a perfect day for trudging.

Today marks the ninth time I've worked with Harry. That means that after today, I only have one more hour to go. Ten service hours is all I need for this semester. And since, let's face it, I haven't exactly helped Harry much, I'm going to do something else next semester. Like picking up garbage in the park. It's hard to let anybody down when you're picking up garbage. That way Mrs. Winnegan can find someone better to help Harry without actually having to fire me. I wonder if anyone has actually been fired from service hours before.

Maybe it's because I'm staring at my shoes while I walk that I don't see him coming. By the time it registers in my brain that the slap-slap sound of sneakers hitting the floor is heading toward me—right toward me—it's too late. I lift my chin at the exact moment Harry runs full-steam into my chest. And just like Newton's First Law of Motion says, an object in motion stays in motion. Harry does. And he takes me with him.

I lie on the hallway floor gasping for air and flexing my arms and legs to check for broken bones. Harry bounces back up and starts talking—fast, arms and hands flying.

"Gabe! Gabe! You won't believe it. I got four out of five. Four out of five!" He hops from one foot to the other.

I roll over so I'm on all fours. I estimate my lungs are back to working at around 45% capacity, so it's safe to get up. Using the wall for leverage, I pull myself up and stand against the wall. Leaving plenty of space between me and Harry.

"What?" I ask. The words have been pouring out of Harry, but I'm not sure my oxygen-deprived brain actually took any of them in.

He bounds across the hall and socks me in the arm. Ow.

"My spelling test! Gabe, I got four out of five right."

"You did?" My jaw goes slack with shock.

"I did. I really did. I asked Mrs. Winnegan to double check because I didn't believe her."

If Harry smiles any bigger, his face is going to split in two.

"Let me see." It's not that I don't believe Harry, I just want to see it for myself. Four out of five right? That's 80%. That's like a B-. A solid, respectable grade for any kid. And a "wow" kind of grade on a spelling test for Harry.

"I left it on my desk. Let's go."

So I let Harry drag me down the hall by my right arm. The same arm that last year—thanks to a locker that wouldn't open and a really heavy rolling backpack—was 1/8 of an inch longer than my left for a while. But today I don't care. Which is a good thing since Harry's pulling so hard and so fast that by the time we get there I might be able to scratch my ankle without bending over.

When we get to the classroom, Mrs. Winnegan is sitting on her desk waiting for us. Her smile is almost as big as Harry's.

"How about this, Gabe?" She waves a piece of paper at me. It's Harry's test. And sure enough, it says 4/5 across the top. In purple ink. With five exclamation points. And two stickers. Clearly, this spelling test is a big deal.

"I know, it's great!" I say.

Harry's bouncing around next to me and goes to slug me in the arm again. The same arm. I duck and somehow manage to turn it into more of a fist bump. Then I maneuver my body until I'm on the other side of the desk from Harry. That much excitement is dangerous.

"I mean, I know I didn't get them all right. I still spelled hamburger wrong—but that's almost like a challenge word anyway, right, Mrs. Winnegan?"

She nods and smiles one of those proud smiles my mom gives me when I hold the door open for an old lady on the way into church.

"Four out of five is outstanding. It's amazing. It's stupendous." I make huge, sweeping arm gestures, making Harry laugh. "Really, Harry, that's huge. As for hamburger, we'll get it. Don't worry."

Harry's bouncing and jumping turns slightly more frantic.

"Hey, Mrs. Winnegan, can I go to the bathroom? I've gotta go."

"Go right ahead."

Harry pounds out the door and down the hall. Mrs. Winnegan waits until we can't hear him anymore.

"Thank you, Gabe."

"For what?"

"For this." She points at Harry's test.

"I didn't think I was helping." I scratch my head. "It didn't seem like it was working. Last time he got most of the words wrong."

"But it *was* helping. And I could see it was." She stands up and walks to the window. "I watched the two of you in the courtyard. With the sidewalk chalk. Harry was having fun."

"I guess so."

"So this time, for this test, I took him out into the courtyard while everyone else was at an assembly. And I let him spell the words first on the sidewalk—with chalk—and then transfer them onto the paper. And this is what happened. Four out of five, Gabe. He got four out of five."

Her voice goes all wobbly at the end. She's going to cry. I'm terrible with crying. I never know what to do. And I sure don't know what to do when a teacher cries. So I do the only thing I can think of. I bolt.

"I'm going to wait for Harry out in the courtyard, okay?"

Mrs. Winnegan nods before she reaches behind her for a tissue and blows her nose with a giant honk.

Harry must've really had to go or else he's stopping and telling anyone who's left in the building about his test. Whatever the reason, he's gone for a long time. I pull out my tessellation and work on it a bit more. I stare at what I've got. I've triple checked every line and every angle. It's a perfect semiregular tessellation. A perfectly boring semiregular tessellation. And quadruple checking all of it isn't going to change that.

Harry plops onto the bench next to me. "Cool."

"Yeah?"

"Yeah. Really cool. It kind of looks like . . ."

"What?" That's been my whole problem. To me, it doesn't look like anything but a bunch of math.

Harry turns his head from side to side, then stands up and looks straight down at it. "It does. It looks like a spider web. A really cool spider web."

"A spider web?" I mimic Harry's movements, but it doesn't matter how much I move my head or whether I look at it from above or below, I don't get it.

"Yeah. Like if you colored it in. Make the web parts kind of a shimmery silver color and the between parts green like a leaf or brown like the wood on a fence. It'd look just like a spider web."

Harry's fingers sketch in the air while he talks. And all of a sudden, I do. I see it.

"If you want, I could loan you my best fake spider. It's a brown recluse and it totally looks real," he says.

"Uh, okay."

Could a spider web tessellation with a fake spider be art? Sister Stevie says art makes you feel something. Spiders make me feel scared. And itchy.

It could work.

When Harry spells hamburger right three times in a row, we're done. He races ahead of me to show his test to his mom. I pause in front of Mrs. Winnegan's desk to have her sign my service hours sheet.

"One more to go, huh?" she says without looking up.

"Yeah." I scuff at the floor with the toe of my shoe. "Would it be okay if I kept coming?"

"You mean after the ten hours are done?"

I nod.

"It would be more than okay." Mrs. Winnegan reaches for another tissue. I race out of the room almost as fast as Harry did.

Twenty

I look out the front window in time to see Maya ride past my house again. That's the fourth time. Each time it looks like she's going to turn into the driveway, but at the last minute she swerves back into the street. Is she waiting for me to come outside? Or getting her courage up to come to the door?

Unlike me, Maya never has problems in the courage department. I guess that must mean she's waiting for me to come out. I pull on a sweatshirt and jam my feet into a pair of sneakers. By the time I open the front door, she's at the end of the block again. A quick turn and she's heading back my way. I know the moment she sees me. There's a hitch in her pedaling. I don't say anything or even wave. I just walk down the steps and our front walk until I reach the curb at the same time she brings her bike to a stop.

"Hey." Maya's chewing on her lower lip. Any strawberry gloss that was there is gone now. And her bangs have slipped out of the sparkly clip and are hanging down into her eyes. She looks like Maya again.

"Hey."

"I was wondering how your interview went."

What? *That's* what she wants to talk about?

"Well, I was wondering why you kissed Linc."

She lets out a huge breath, blowing her bangs straight up in the air.

"Yeah, me too."

"What does that even mean?" It's starting to rain. Well, more like something between a mist and a drizzle. "How can you *not* know why? *You're* the one who did the kissing. I saw you."

"I know you did."

"So why'd you do it?"

"I was mad at you." She says it like that's the whole answer.

"Okay, first why were you mad at me this time? What did I do?" I pull my sleeves down over my hands. The sun is starting to set and it's getting cold.

Maya stares down the street. "I always thought you would be my first kiss." More lip chewing. "But last year you were crazy about Becca and then this year, even when I changed stuff about me, you didn't seem to notice."

"Yeah, I did."

"You did?"

"Yep. Hair, lip gloss, sideways looks I didn't understand—all of it."

"I didn't think you noticed." She'd already said that.

"So you kissed Linc?"

"Shelby told me I needed to do something to get your attention."

"Shelby said?"

"Yeah."

"So you kissed Linc."

Maya looks at me for the first time since she stopped her bike. She grins.

"Well, it kind of worked, didn't it?"

A laugh spurts out of me before I can stop it. Before I can remember I'm mad at her. Then it's me chewing on my lip. And staring down at my sneakers. "I guess I kind of always thought you'd be my first kiss, too."

"Really?"

Neither of us says anything for what feels like a really

long time but what is probably no more than twelve seconds.

"So how long do you think it'll take you to forget about kissing Linc?" I look up. "If you want to forget it, I mean."

"I do." Maya unzips and rezips her jacket twice. "I kind of already have."

More not talking.

"See you tomorrow?" she asks.

"Sure."

Maya gives me a fluttery-finger wave and pedals away. I stand there until way after I can't see her any more, then head for my house. And dinner.

Me kissing Maya. Someday.

I trip over a crack in the sidewalk and almost fall on my face. Almost.

My mom said I absolutely, positively had to clean up the "mess" on top of my desk before dinner. And even though I could make a strong case for a couple—mostly neat—stacks of paper not actually being a mess, I'm hungry. And I want dinner. So if putting some papers into a drawer means getting food faster, that's what I'll do.

Halfway through one stack I find my "application

checklist," with all the important dates on the way to an acceptance from CSMHS. The one that used to hang on my wall. Until the interview happened. Underneath it are three scraps of paper. The "yeses."

After I got back from my interview, I took the checklist and stuffed it into the middle of a bunch of other papers. It's not like it mattered when I'd get the next letter. It wasn't going to be the fourth yes.

Still, I read the last line. The date the final decisions will be made. It's two days away. Two days.

Wait. They haven't made the final decisions yet. So maybe it's *not* too late. Maybe?

All of a sudden I know. This is one of those moments. One of those times when I could either sit back and not do something, or I could take action. Linc is always talking about taking action. And of course, he usually means with girls. But maybe *I* should take action right now. Maybe it's time for me to do something bold.

I'm going back to CSMHS.

It's not over yet.

The weirdest thing happens. I feel completely calm. My palms aren't sweating. My pits aren't either. And my stomach? Not even a tiny clench. I don't know if it's my grandpa or Saint Jude—he and I have been talking a lot lately—or the Holy Spirit. Maybe all three. All I do know is something—or someone—is guiding me. Sort of pointing the way. I'll have to be the one to do it, but at least I know what to do.

I bust out of my room and nearly run my mom over.

"Mom, can you do me a huge favor?"

"What is it?"

"Can you take me to CSMHS tomorrow afternoon? See, I messed up my first interview. I didn't mean to—I promise I didn't—but I messed it up. And I'm pretty sure I can fix it. Only I have to go there tomorrow. It'll mean missing last period, but it's just a review for next week's test. But I have to miss it so I can get back in time for the art show. Will you take me?" I run out of breath and slump against the wall.

My mom's face does not transform itself into the *can-do* look she always gets when I ask for help. She loves solving problems—especially mine or Sabrina's. But no *can-do* look now.

"Oh, honey. I wish I could. But I'm catering a funeral reception at church. It's my first one. I'm providing all of the desserts and they asked me to serve, too."

"Oh."

"I'm really sorry, honey."

"It's okay, Mom." It's not like it's her fault that someone died and she can't help me. I can tell she feels rotten about it.

"Can you ask Dad?"

"Sure."

"And let me know what he says." My mom grabs my hand and squeezes—hard. "Don't worry. We'll figure something out."

I find my dad tearing lettuce for salads. I tell him my whole spiel and wait for him to say "Of course I'll take you. No problem." But that's not what he says.

"Tomorrow, Champ?"

"Yeah, it has to be tomorrow." Any later and it will be too late.

"I'm sorry, but I can't."

"You can't?"

"No. I've got a new patient coming late in the afternoon."

"Can't you reschedule?"

My dad stops tearing lettuce and looks at me. "My new patient is a five-year-old girl who was badly burned in an accident. I'm going to help her try to walk tomorrow. It's going to be really hard—and really painful for her."

"Oh."

"Did you ask Mom?"

"She can't take me either."

My dad hands me the placemats and I start to set the table.

"I'm really sorry, Gabe."

"It's okay."

My plan probably wouldn't have worked anyway.

"Hey, what about Grandma?"

"Huh?"

"What about Grandma? I'm sure she could help."

And before I can say anything about how it's probably hopeless anyway, and how even if it isn't hopeless I'm not sure that having Grandma along with her superpowers that make me spill my guts all over the place even if I don't mean to is really all that helpful, my dad dials the phone and says hello.

The phone call is over before I get the table set.

"Problem solved." My dad rubs his hands together. "Grandma will pick you up from school and take you straight there. Pretty good, huh?" He grins.

"Yeah, pretty good." I smile, too.

The plan is back on.

Twenty-one

Since we're leaving before the end of the school day, my grandma has to come to the office to sign me out. She beats me there and, when I walk in, she is in the middle of a conversation with Mrs. Francisco about training for her next marathon.

"Ready, Grandma?"

Grandma turns and smiles. "Sure, honey. Let's go." She waves to Mrs. Francisco and we start to head for the front door together. When I follow her outside, the first thing I notice is the complete absence of any clouds. The sun is so bright that at first I think maybe I'm not actually seeing what I think I'm seeing.

"Grandma?"

"I'm sorry, honey. When I went out to the garage, my car wouldn't start. I think it's the battery."

"So?"

Grandma slings her arm around my shoulders and grins. "So it's you, me, and the cycle."

Yeah. Because just going to CSMHS and throwing myself at them to beg for another chance isn't humiliating enough. Now I'm going to arrive on a motorcycle with my grandma. I won't actually be riding *on* the motorcycle, though. No, I'll be in the sidecar.

"Come on, honey. It'll be fun."

Grandma and I sit outside Dr. Tremaine's office while he decides whether or not he'll let me talk to him. That's not exactly what the school secretary said, but I'm pretty sure that's what "let me see if he's expecting you" means.

I got to school super early this morning and waited outside Mrs. Capistrano's office until she got there. Then I told her what happened during my interview—all of it. I think she's kind of like a priest or a lawyer. When you tell her stuff, she has to keep it a secret. Well, unless it's something that could hurt someone else. And me blowing my interview and showing The Flog to Dr. McNeely and Dr. Tremaine didn't hurt anyone. Except me.

After I finished my horrible, embarrassing story, Mrs. Capistrano said she'd call and plead my case. She's usually great at convincing people—she convinced Linc's parents to let him try out for basketball, and I didn't think that would ever happen. I just hope she was as good at talking Dr. Tremaine into giving me another chance.

"Do you think your mom would mind if I hosted Thanksgiving dinner?"

"What?"

"Thanksgiving, Gabe," says my grandma. "It's next week."

"I know."

"So do you think your mom would mind if we had Thanksgiving at my house this year?"

"I don't know. I guess not." Which is not at all what I'm thinking. What I'm really thinking is why are you asking me about Thanksgiving dinner when I'm waiting to find out if I get the chance to unscrewup a really big screwup? But I don't say that. Because she's my grandma. And because she drove me all the way here, even if I did have to ride in the sidecar.

So I nod and keep nodding while Grandma keeps talking. Her voice is like a mosquito buzzing in my ear, but it's not quite loud enough to hear the actual words over the pounding of my heart. I rub my medal through my shirt, praying to everybody I can think of. I ask Grandpa to help me if he can—after I tell him (again) how sorry I am for messing up in the first place. The buzzing keeps going.

"I was thinking that instead of a regular Thanksgiving dinner with turkey and all that, I'd just serve pie."

What? That was weird enough to break through my counting and praying and hoping.

"Just pie?" There's no way my mom is saying yes to this.

"Yep. Just pie. Different varieties, but all pies. You know Thanksgiving was Grandpa's favorite holiday."

I know. It's mine, too.

"And his favorite part of the meal was the pie. Pumpkin, of course. And pecan. But really he loved any kind of pie." Grandma stares down at her hands and twirls her wedding rings around and around.

"I've been making a pie every week since he died. His favorites and some we never got a chance to try." I guess that explains why she brings pie whenever she comes for dinner. "So what do you think?"

"Pies would be good." I don't want to lie to her, though. "Mom might still bring a turkey."

She chuckles and glances over at Dr. Tremaine's door. Two seconds later, it swings open. She really does have magical powers.

Dr. Tremaine's voice—at least I think it's his voice—calls from inside. "Mr. Carpenter, you have five minutes."

Mr. Carpenter.

Five minutes.

I rub my hand over the top of my head. The ridges are still there. The inside of my motorcycle helmet, with all its grooves and indentations, left its impression on my hair. My poufy, uncontrollable hair now looks kind of like a brain. I try to look at the bright side. Dr. Tremaine is a scientist. That must mean he likes brains, right?

When I walk into Dr. Tremaine's office, I'm surprised to see Dr. McNeely leaning against the wall. He smiles and nods, but doesn't say anything.

Dr. Tremaine doesn't smile or nod. But he doesn't seem mad either. Mostly he just looks curious. "The floor is yours."

"Okay. Well, thank you for letting me talk to you." I concentrate really hard on ignoring the clenching in my stomach. "I know I messed up the last time I was here."

Silence.

"Um, the question I was supposed to answer with my presentation was about how science and math helped me solve a problem. And I think I mostly did that."

More silence. But Dr. McNeely nods again, which I hope means it's okay to keep going.

"See, science and math did help me with basketball. They helped me understand and analyze all the different parts of the game, and that got me the job with the team. But the other notebook you saw—the stuff about . . . well, gas—that helps me, too." Dr. McNeely raises an eyebrow—just one. "That notebook was way at the bottom of my bag. Or at least it was supposed to be. But when I pulled my presentation out, I guess I grabbed it, too. See, I was keeping all that data so I could figure out how to solve an embarrassing problem. It was supposed to be just for me." I scrunch up my face. "I ended up embarrassing myself worse than ever."

Dr. McNeely snickers and even Dr. Tremaine cracks the tiniest of smiles.

"But I didn't want you to think that I was trying to make a joke. The problem isn't a joke. And me wanting to come to school here is not a joke. I *really* want to be here next year." My voice cracks. I clear my throat—twice—and keep going. There's more to say. "I want to study and learn and hang out with other kids who like science and math as much as I do. I want to join the Meteorology Club and try out for the Academic Olympics team. I want to find out how much stuff I don't know yet and then try to learn it."

Dr. Tremaine looks down at his watch.

"Thank you, Gabe."

My five minutes are up. But I said most of what I rehearsed on the way over, so that's okay.

"Um, thank you, sir. Both of you sirs."

One good thing—make that the only good thing—about being driven back to school in my grandma's sidecar is that she can't ask me a bunch of questions about how it went. Instead, I sit with my eyes—and mouth—slammed shut. I stop worrying about getting to the art show on time and instead worry about getting there in one piece. My eyes are shut because my grandma is not what you'd call a cautious driver. Anytime I get brave enough to open my eyes, something happens that makes me close them again. And my mouth is shut because of the bugs. Every few minutes I hear—or worse, feel—a bug smack against the face shield of my helmet. A big, juicy-sounding one hit a few minutes ago. I'm not going to look. But I am going to make sure none of them end up in my mouth.

Finally, we pull up in front of St. Jude. I whip off my helmet and grab my briefcase out of the storage trunk. When I check my watch, I've got five minutes to spare. The art show starts in five minutes. I'm supposed to be standing next to my project right now. But I don't move from the spot where I'm standing.

"Gabe? Are you okay, honey? I know that last turn was a doozy." Grandma chuckles. Yeah. Lots of the turns were "doozies," but that's not why I'm still standing here.

"Thanks, Grandma. For everything."

She grabs me and gives me one of her special hugs. The ones where she squeezes so hard you kind of can't breathe and at least some of your bones seem to rub together.

"Our Gabe." It's her way of letting me know Grandpa is here, too. He always called me "my Gabe." She pats my cheek like Grandpa always did and then gives me one last squeeze. "I'm going to find a parking spot; then I'll be right in. Now hurry, you're already late."

And I am late. There are a bunch of littler kids packing the hall. Sister Stevie said Mrs. Quincy always invites the kids from St. Jude Elementary to come over and see the show. I asked her to make extra sure Mrs. Winnegan's class came. There's something I want Harry to see.

I follow the pack of kids into our cafeteria, part of which has been transformed into an art gallery. The walls are covered with shiny drapes in all different shades of blue. Some art work hangs on these drapes and others are displayed on long tables. There are spotlights on some of the paintings. And there's music playing—some of the classical stuff Sister Stevie likes to play for us when we're supposed to be stretching our minds. If you ignore the faint aroma of today's beef stroganoff (and if you can, you should), it feels a lot like what I think an actual art gallery might be like. It doesn't sound like one—there's too much talking and laughing and shuffling and not enough whispering—but it's still pretty cool.

I hang back for a minute, checking it all out without being seen. Then I slide in with a group of fifth graders who are taking a tour of all the exhibits. I'm not much taller than most of them—and not at all taller than two of them—so it's pretty easy to blend in.

Some of the projects by Mrs. Quincy's honor students are just wow. Paintings of flowers and trees—and people—that actually look just like what they're supposed to. I could *never* do that. Someone else made a sculpture of a pineapple out of strips of recycled soda cans.

It's pretty cool to see that the stuff our class did doesn't look too out of place. Shelby's is incredible. She did a tessellation. But instead of just drawing it on paper and coloring it, she carved it in clay, then glazed and fired it.

Spencer did some crazy hard fractal and Jake and Mary Frances both did drawings that show examples of Fibonacci numbers in nature. And after calling origami a cop-out, Cameron ended up making an origami sailboat that doesn't look much more difficult than Linc's goofy pirate hat.

When we get to the end of the displays, I step out from behind the tallest fifth grader who I was using as my human shield.

"Hey, guys."

"Hey," Linc and Maya say together. They both chose origami. And both of their projects look really cool.

"What do you think?" Maya asks.

"It looks great." She made an origami tree. It's tall and the branches stretch up and out gracefully.

"It's *our* tree," she says. "Look closer."

I bend down and examine it closely. It's then I see them. Two tiny people, perched in the tree, one sitting two branches higher than the other.

"It's perfect."

Maya smiles at me with her whole face. My own face feels hot and my palms start to sweat, just a little bit.

"What about mine?" Linc smacks me in the arm. "Check this out. It's an origami catapult."

"I can see that."

"Watch this." He takes a wadded up piece of paper, places it carefully onto one part of his creation, and flicks it with his finger. The arm of the catapult follows a perfect arc, sending the paper wad sailing through the air where it lands on Sister Stevie's head. She plucks it from the folds of her veil and brings it over, handing it to Linc.

"Hi, Sister. Sorry I'm late," I say. Earlier today, I'd let Sister Stevie know where I was going—and why.

She puts her hand on my shoulder and raises her eyebrows.

I shrug. "I don't know. Won't know for a couple weeks. But I did everything I could."

She smiles. "I'll be praying."

"Me, too."

All of a sudden my left arm is yanked nearly out of its socket. I look behind me and see Harry. And the rest of his class. But it's Harry who is trying to separate my arm from the rest of my body.

"Gabe! Did you see it? Did you?"

"See what?"

"Our spider web. Did you see it yet?"

He stops pulling my arm long enough to point. And there it is. Hanging on the wall. Our spider web. It's the tessellation I worked so hard on that never looked like anything more than lines and angles to me. But Harry was right. It really does look like a spider web. I found the perfect kind of paint for the web itself. When the sun hits it—like it is now—it shimmers and reflects prisms of light.

The background looks even better. Sister Stevie said it was okay if Harry worked on it with me. So after school one day, instead of me helping him with spelling, he helped me figure out how to make it look like the web was spun on a leaf. We used a bunch of different shades of green. Harry was in charge of sketching out the veins in the leaf. The best part—according to Harry—is the brown recluse spider that we glued onto the web.

The best part—according to me—is the sign next to our project.

The Spider's Web

Artist: Gabe Carpenter

Co-Artist: Harry Newton

"Can I take a picture of you two artists with your work?" asks Mrs. Winnegan.

So Harry stands on one side and I stand on the other. All the kids in his class crowd in behind Mrs. Winnegan, looking like they want to be in the picture, too. When I glance over at Harry, he's standing very straight and very still. And he's smiling with everything he's got.

Click.

Twenty-two

Is my tie straight? I can't tell. My dad said the knot is supposed to be in line with my chin. And I think it might be. But since I have to duck between Linc and Flick to get anywhere near the mirror, it's hard to be sure.

"Go, Jaguars!" Flick yells and slaps both me and Linc on the back before he heads out of the locker room. No way is my tie straight anymore.

"We look pretty good, huh?" Linc asks.

"Yeah."

He beams at me and I grin back. Linc in a green and gold St. Jude uniform—number eight. And me in a dress shirt, tie, and church pants. Because that's what the coaching staff wears.

"So . . ." I flip through my notes. Stuff about our guys and who's doing what. And stuff about the other team. It's all here. I'm ready. Really ready. It's time to be out there. For me and for Linc, too.

"Gabe?"

"Yeah?"

"This is going to be awesome."

"Yeah."

More grinning at each other in the mirror. I try to fix my hair and Linc flexes his biceps one more time. Then the whistle blows—Coach Schwimmer's get-out-here-right-now whistle—and we, the last two guys in the locker room, run out to join the rest of the team. Together.

Linc's right. Sitting on the bench with the team and the coaches, watching the game from that close, keeping the stats, being part of the huddles. It *is* awesome. All of it.

In the end, the St. Jude Jaguars win by three points. That makes us undefeated.

When I get home, I go straight to my room. And waiting for me in the middle of my bed is an envelope. A dark blue envelope addressed to me. It's from CSMHS. This time there's no note from my mom. This time she didn't open it first.

I glance over at my nightstand. Next to my alarm clock sits a picture of me and Grandpa at the beach. Grandma was there, too—on the other side of the camera. Grandpa and I are smiling and squinting into the sun; his arm is looped around my shoulders. I can almost feel the squeeze.

After taking a steadying breath, I flip the envelope over and slip my finger under the flap. It opens easily and a single piece of paper, folded precisely into thirds, falls out. I read it through once, then go back to the top and start again.

There's a gentle knock on my door. It's already open.

"Well?" my mom and dad ask together.

"I need to call Grandma."

I bolt out of my room and down the hall, nearly flattening Sabrina.

"Gabe!"

The three of them follow me into the kitchen. I punch number two on speed dial and wait for Grandma to answer. Then I tell them all, together.

"They said yes."

Marilee Haynes lives with her husband and three young children just outside Charlotte, North Carolina. A full-time stay-at-home mom, she writes middle grade fiction in stolen quiet moments (in other words, when everyone else is asleep). *Genius under Construction* is the sequel to Haynes's critically acclaimed first novel, *a.k.a. Genius*, which was published by Pauline Teen in 2013.

Find out how it all started
in a.k.a. Genius

What readers are saying...

"*A.K.A. Genius* is a witty and entertaining story that tells the life of a middle school boy as he tries to survive the drama of middle school. Gabe could be the kid sitting next to me in class, or I could see myself in his shoes as parts of the story unfold. Middle school can be a rough journey for a kid and the author does a great job at inserting humor to make light of situations."

—Sean L., 13, attends a public middle school in Michigan

"*A.K.A. Genius* is a good book because it deals with situations that kids like me go through every day—like trying to do well at school or getting along with your friends and family. A lot of the things that happened to Gabe made me laugh, and there were definitely some surprises, too. I think lots of kids will find something to like about this book because the situations are funny, embarrassing, stressful, happy, sad, and exciting...just like real life."

—Charlie B., 10, attends a Catholic school in North Carolina

Catholic Fiction

Pauline Teen brings you books you'll love!
We promise you stories that

✍ make you laugh—and sometimes cry

✍ make you think and help you dream

✍ let you explore the real world

At Pauline, we love a good story and the long
tradition of Christian fiction. Our books are fun
to read. And the stories will engage your faith
by accepting who you are *here* and *now* while
inspiring you to recognize who God *calls you to
become.*

Pauline TEEN
Growing up with faith

self-acceptance/giftedness/humor

a.k.a. genius

GAS

Girls

Marilee Haynes

Genius
under construction

Marilee Haynes

gifts and limitations/service/humor

immigration/communism/adventure

LIZETTE M. LANTIGUA

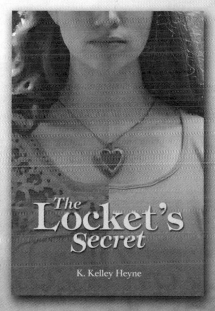

The
Locket's
Secret

K. Kelley Heyne

family/fantasy/grief

Praying
with the
Holy
Father

Adoring Jesus
with the
Holy
Father

Honoring
Mary
with the
Holy
Father

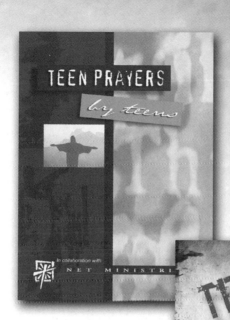

Pauline TEEN

Who: The Daughters of St. Paul

What: Pauline Teen—linking your life to Jesus Christ and his Church

When: 24/7

Where: All over the world and on www.pauline.org

Why: Because our life-long passion is to witness to God's amazing love for all people!

How: Inspiring lives of holiness through Apps, digital media, concerts, websites, social media, videos, blogs, books, music albums, rad media literacy, DVDs, ebooks, stores, conferences, bookfairs parish exhibits, personal conta illustration, vocation talks, ph iting, editing, graphic desig

BOOKS & MEDIA

The Daughters of St. Paul operate book and media centers at the following addresses. Visit, call, or write the one nearest you today, or find us at www.pauline.org.

CALIFORNIA
3908 Sepulveda Blvd, Culver City, CA 90230   310-397-8676
935 Brewster Avenue, Redwood City, CA 94063   650-369-4230
5945 Balboa Avenue, San Diego, CA 92111   858-565-9181

FLORIDA
145 SW 107th Avenue, Miami, FL 33174   305-559-6715

HAWAII
1143 Bishop Street, Honolulu, HI 96813   808-521-2731
Neighbor Islands call: 866-521-2731

ILLINOIS
172 North Michigan Avenue, Chicago, IL 60601   312-346-4228

LOUISIANA
4403 Veterans Memorial Blvd, Metairie, LA 70006   504-887-7631

MASSACHUSETTS
885 Providence Hwy, Dedham, MA 02026   781-326-5385

MISSOURI
9804 Watson Road, St. Louis, MO 63126   314-965-3512

NEW YORK
64 West 38th Street, New York, NY 10018   212-754-1110

SOUTH CAROLINA
243 King Street, Charleston, SC 29401   843-577-0175

VIRGINIA
1025 King Street, Alexandria, VA 22314   703-549-3806

CANADA
3022 Dufferin Street, Toronto, ON M6B 3T5   416-781-9131

SMILE
God loves you